TRUE PETECTIVES

A YOSHI & GATSBY OMNIBUS

ROBERT J. SMITH

CONTENTS

PETECTIVES™

"The cat is the only animal which accepts the comforts but rejects the bondage of domesticity." - Georges Louis Leclerc de Buffon

CHAPTER 1

It was a clear October night with a big yellow moon hanging in the black sky above me. I was running through the Forest Heights subdivision as fast as four paws could carry me. I had an appointment with a client and I was already late.

"Yo, Gatsby!" a rough voice barked out. "Get over here! I need to talk to you!" To a human ear that would've just sounded like some mean half-crazed bulldog barking at the moon. To me it was a mean, half-crazed bulldog calling me over to make me even later for my appointment. I decided to go over and see what he wanted; there was a chance that it would be worth my while. I trotted over to his backyard. His name was Percy; his fur was a deep, dark brown and he always had an expression as if he'd spent the day guzzling spoilt milk.

"Get your orange butt over here!" he yelled as he saw me approaching. Before I answered him, I made sure that he was chained to his house. The chain was slack but I could tell how far he could get before his teeth could reach me. I stopped about five feet from where I figured the chain would stop him if he wanted to rip me to cat shreds.

I gave him a big smile. "What do you want, Percival?"

"Why don't you come a little closer?"

"Your breath's strong enough from here. You've got to stop drinking out of the toilet. Or at least wait until somebody flushes." Of course if he was loose, I wouldn't have said that. I'd probably have run to Cuba by now.

"You're pretty funny," he growled. "Look, I've got a message for your boss"

"He's not my boss." I responded. "We're partners!"

"Yeah, whatever. You tell Yoshi that I've got a business opportunity to discuss with him."

"That's out. You know darn well that Yoshi is the ultimate indoor cat. You tell me about this opportunity, then I'll tell him and we'll let you know later. That's how it works."

"Whatever. I ain't dealing with errand boys. I can get you boys ten years worth of catnip – Don't screw it up."

I started to walk away. "OK" I called back, "I'll tell him and maybe we'll get back to you. But if I was you, I wouldn't hold your breath. Well, not without gloves and a hazardous waste suit."

His response was insane barking that rang out through the neighborhood, probably waking up all of the humans in the surrounding houses.

My appointment was in front of the white two-story house on the corner with the huge pine tree that seemed to stretch up to the moon. I was hoping that this would lead to an interesting job. I'd been very idle for the last month and the only other jobs we'd been offered this week was either investigating who had knocked over Mr. Bascom's barbeque, leaving a mess of ashes and used charcoal briquettes in his backyard or finding out who had busted into the Rogers family's garage and raided their freezer. Both of those potential cases seemed so boring that

3

staying home and watching Animal Planet seemed like a more productive use of my time.

As I approached the corner, I got at a good look at the cat that I was supposed to meet as she sat there waiting for me. It may have been the full moon shining down on her or it may have been my imagination but she looked better than a big hunk of fish smothered in tartar sauce sitting in a bowl of buttermilk. She was a white cat with black ears and black patches all over including one around her right eye which was especially cute. She was bigger than me, but this much beauty in a bigger serving was not a bad thing. Whatever this cat needed, I was going to get it for her and then she would marry me out of gratitude and we would have lots of good looking kittens.

"Are you Gatsby?" she asked, breaking me out of my daydream.

"That's me. And would you be the lady in need of my services?" After I had said that I thought that I should probably be more specific. "As a detective? Or a bodyguard?"

When I said "bodyguard" she laughed. Even her mocking laughter was musical. I assumed that she didn't think that a small statured cat would make a good bodyguard. After she got to know me better, she's see how wrong she was.

"I'm sorry," She said, probably after seeing the expression on my face. "I'm sure that you're a great bodyguard but it's too late for that. My brother's missing."

Wonderful. Missing kitty cases are never fun. You could work your tail off trying to find somebody and be outdone by a stupid "Have you seen this Cat?" sign on a lamp post.

"OK, why don't we back up? What's your name?"

"Oh, I'm sorry. My name is Molasses. I live over there in that house, and – what are you laughing at?"

Her name was Molasses and she was wondering what I was laughing at. Humans shouldn't be allowed to name their pets. I made out ok, but there were way too many animals out there with ridiculous names. When they needed a name for the kitty, did they go look in their pantry and pick the first thing that they saw? "Nothing. I wasn't laughing. What's your brother's name and what does he look like?"

"His name is Butterscotch." She paused for a second to see if I was going to start giggling. I held it together and she continued, "He's an American shorthair. He's about 10 pounds with short hair. He has a perfect thirty point face and he's mostly white with thick grey stripes in a Mackerel Tabby pattern."

"Is anybody else looking for him?"

She thought about that for a second. "Well our owners are really going crazy looking for him and I told those dogs that patrol the neighborhood, but nobody seems to be getting anywhere."

"When was the last time you saw him?"

"Last week. It was the day before the weekend. We're not supposed to go out, but he knew how to leave the house when he wanted to. He'd go out at least once a week"

"And where was he going?"

"I don't know. We were close, but he would have to have his alone time. Only this time he didn't come back."

"Could he be going to see a girlfriend?"

"No, that I would know about. He was probably just going to gamble at that awful alley – Did you hear that?"

I had heard a dog bark that I didn't recognize. A minute or so before, I'd gotten a whiff of some strange dogs but there was no threat in sight.

"We're okay. Do you have any reason to think that somebody took him?"

"No. There was no trouble at home between our people. We had no – Who are they?"

There were three dogs crossing the street coming towards us. Mean looking pit bulls, if that doesn't go without saying. They were going for rough, tough and menacing and I have to give them credit, they were getting the job done. I couldn't take one of them down, let alone all three.

I gave Molasses more credit. She didn't scream or bolt. She just stood her ground and glanced from me to them.

"Hey, pretty kitty" The lead dog said. "We came to ugly you up. You and your little boyfriend there." His buddies just growled. I could think of at least five good comebacks to that but as Yoshi has often told me, I need to select the proper time and place for smartaleck remarks. With three murderous killing machines a couple of yards away from us, I was going to need to use my head to do more than come up with witticisms.

CHAPTER 2

The three Pit Bulls were all growling and there was no doubt that if they got us, we'd be ripped to shreds. I whispered to Molasses, "Head up the tree! Now!"

There was a huge, towering evergreen tree fifteen feet behind us. Molasses instantly spun around and headed for it. The dogs bolted towards us. I let my instincts take over. My back went up, my tail went straight up and fluffed up and I let go with a hiss louder than I thought I was capable of. The dogs stopped dead in their tracks, long enough for Molasses to make it to the tree. Yoshi had told me that the meaner a bully, the more easily frightened they were. I spun around and headed after Molasses. They were right on top of me, but I had enough of a head start that I could leap for the tree before they could catch me. I did feel the snip of a dog's teeth just barely touching my tail. Then I was heading up the tree with the three dogs barking and jumping up the trunk, unable to climb after me. Molasses was waiting for me on a high limb. I joined her and we both ran across a branch and then jumped down to the roof of the house.

I heard the front door of the house open and a man's voice yelled, "Hey you dogs, get on out of here!" There was another barrage of angry barks and the door slammed.

At this point we were safely on the roof. She looked at me "Well, I guess you proved me wrong for laughing when you said you could be a bodyguard. I can't believe the way you held off those three killers by yourself!"

"Yeah, my girlish screams held them off long enough for us to escape."

"Whatever! That had to be the bravest thing I've ever seen in my life!" She seemed genuinely impressed. "Let me know what you find out!" She got a running start and then jumped over to roof of the next house. After doing the same for a couple of other houses, she was gone.

It then occurred to me that when she said that was the bravest thing she'd ever seen, I should've replied "You ain't seen nothing yet, baby" or something cool like that. Oh well, I wouldn't want to thrill her too much on our first meeting. Always leave them wanting more.

The next morning was a Monday. The people that I lived with had been home for two days straight and spent the morning dazed and frantic, trying to get out of the house for work and school. This was a hilarious sight that I usually looked forward to but I was a little short on sleep so I napped through it all. They were usually gone by 8:00. A few minutes after 9:00, I was going over the previous nights events with Yoshi. We were in the master bedroom where Yoshi liked to take his morning nap. He had his sixteen pound body perched on the woman's pillow as if it were his own. I was sitting on the floor next to the bed looking up at him. Yoshi was completely black from head to tail, except for a few white hairs on his chest and his bright yellow eyes. His eyes were almond shaped and had been so prominent when he was a kitten that they made him look like a Siamese cat which is why our owners had given him an Asian name. As he grew, the resemblance to a Siamese cat went away but he kept the name. I never knew why they had named me "Gatsby", although I know that there's a famous book titled, "The Great

Gatsby". I've always assumed that everybody just understood how great I am and they gave me a name to match. Yoshi's always saying that if they had given me a better name that I might have a humbler attitude.

I'd told Yoshi everything that happened last night from Percy's request to our beautiful client's missing brother to being chased by the gang of pit bulls. Although he looked sleepy, I knew he was paying attention to every detail. He always waited until I was finished to ask his questions. "What on earth does that dog want from me?" he asked.

"I don't know. Knowing him, it's probably some kind of criminal activity. We should just blow him off and concentrate on Mo's case."

"Mo?" His left eyebrow whiskers rose.

"I mean Molasses. Miss Molasses. Our new client, who I am treating with the utmost respect and professionalism." I smiled my cutest cat smile.

He sighed. "You're not getting overly familiar with a client again, are you? Has your collar even dried yet from all the tears you cried when that Siamese dumped you last week? And it was just last month that you were acting heartbroken when that Gwendolyn moved away."

"Look, I'm a professional. I'm not going to ask her to marry me until I've found her brother. Now, are you going to lay up there and comment on my love life all morning or do you have instructions?"

"Of course. First, you can stress to Percy that I'm not visiting him so any communication will need to go through you. I would've thought that everyone in the neighborhood would know that by now, but apparently not. On the Butterscotch matter, you'll need to make the usual inquiries. Also, talk to Duke and see if he knows anything about those thugs that attacked you last night. They give an interesting twist to what should be a routine missing pet case."

"Twist? What twist? They were a bunch of thugs that thought they'd bully a couple of innocent cats."

He glanced at the alarm clock on the end table next to the bed. It was 9:52. Eight minutes until the mid-morning nap. Yoshi's mid-morning nap was not to be interrupted, postponed or cancelled for any reason short of the end of the world and even then under protest. I had to hurry him up. "Do you have any instructions that might actually help find this missing cat?"

"Do I really need to instruct you on that? It's going to be a pain, although Molasses did say something that might make things go easier although I need to think about that for a little while. In the meantime, you're going to have to canvas the area for a couple miles, asking every animal you encounter if they've seen him. Get help from your rat friend if you must and –"

He was interrupted by a flurry of barking coming from the side of the house. We both ran from the bedroom and went downstairs to the kitchen. Actually I ran. Yoshi walked after me. The kitchen window was half open and I could jump up on the windowsill to see what was going on. The window looked out on the house next door and the grass in-between. Sitting on the grass and barking at us was Duke, a 75 pound German Shepherd.

I greeted him. "Hey Duke."

"Hiya, kid." He had a gruff personality but was usually friendly to me. "I need you to-"

The words were hardly out of his mouth before Yoshi had jumped on the windowsill next to me and interrupted. "We don't work for you! Shouldn't you be out harassing the mailman?"

"Its ten o'clock. Shouldn't you be unconscious?" Yoshi's schedule was well known. "I didn't come to see you; I need to talk with Gatsby." Duke said in a deep growl. His gruff personality usually got a lot gruffer when Yoshi was around.

Yoshi didn't care for Duke either and from the look on his face, he was about to tell Duke exactly what he thought of him. Then he yawned. It was ten o'clock. He jumped down off the windowsill, told me to "Handle it." and trotted back to the bedroom.

I looked back at Duke. "So, what can I do for you?"

"I need to show you something. Can you take a walk with me?"

"Sure, but I'm not bringing my pooper scooper."

"Come on. Let's go!" This time the deep growl was for me. Duke was not noted for his appreciation of dog humor. I went outside to join him.

Duke had been in the police K-9 corps for five years and after being injured in the line of duty had been forced to retire to the suburbs. He set himself and three other dogs up as the cops of the neighborhood. They patrolled and performed duties like harassing suspicious strangers, keeping feral animals away and stopping pets from pooping on the sidewalks. Yoshi and I were both super secret special honorary members of Duke's police force. Duke wanted us to become full members but we had declined. We were a little too independent minded to be expected to follow orders.

"Where are we going?" I said when I caught up to him.

"Not far." Was all the answer I got. He trotted off over the lawn and up the sidewalk with me right on his heels. It was a very nice day for mid-October with a warm temperature and a sunny sky. Some of the houses had Jack O'Lanterns on their porches and Halloween decorations in their windows. Yoshi always found the black cat decorations to be horribly offensive. At this time of the day most people were at work so that the streets were clear and everything was quiet. After we'd gone a couple of blocks in silence, Duke looked back at me and said, "So kid, I heard you had a little dust-up last night."

"How did you hear about that?"

"The night has a thousand eyes, kid. A little bird told me about three tough pit bulls being backed off by a little orange cat. I only know of one orange cat around here with that much nerve."

"OK, I'll admit to that. They came from out of nowhere. I had never seen those dogs before. Do you know anything about them?"

"No. But I have heard a rumor about dogfighting in the area."

That took me by surprise. "Dogfighting? Get out! Not in this neighborhood!"

"Crime has no area code, kid."

Yes, he actually talked like that. I didn't know exactly what the injury was that made him retire, but when he said things like that I suspected that had something to do with his head.

"OK", I said. "Where do I go to find this dogfighting?"

"If I knew that, I'd have shut them down by now!" He growled.

"Of course. Well, if I run into them again, I'll follow them to wherever they came from and let you know."

His head snapped around. "If you see them again, you run and get me quick!" He paused and looked up. "Here we are. Follow me."

We had stopped outside a two-story grey house.

The second-in-command of the Dog Patrol was Preston, another big bodied German Shepherd who was a little bigger than Duke but he was less muscular and more fat. He was sitting next to a smoke-grey cat who had obviously just been through a rough time. The cat was bruised, battered and beaten. His left eye was swollen shut, his right ear was cut and there were claw

18

marks on his back and his chest. Other than that he looked good. Despite his injuries, he stood up straight and tall and had a regal attitude, like he owned the place.

As we approached I gave Preston a nod. He nodded back. I looked at the grey cat. "What happened, man? You look like I feel."

He responded "Well, if you're Gatsby you're the one who should look like this."

"Excuse me?"

Preston spoke up "Why don't we back up and make introductions? Then we can talk about why he looks like this." Preston was usually a voice of reason. "Gatsby, this little guy's name is Smokey. Smokey, you were right, this is Gatsby. Now why don't you tell Gatsby what you told me and the chief?"

"Fine I'll talk to the fleabag."

I spoke "That's nice, but how about you do it without the name-calling?"

Smokey was still scowling at me. "I was minding my own business last night and these three dogs jumped on me. I couldn't get away, they had me surrounded. After they beat me down, they asked me if I knew a cat named Gatsby. I said no and they told me to find him and tell him to back off."

I knew the answer to my next question but I asked it anyway. "Back off of what?"

"I don't know. I don't know who you are or who those dogs are or why they almost beat me to death or why I have to be your messenger boy."

"Can you describe these dogs?"

He did and there was no doubt about it, they were the same dogs that harassed me earlier last night. They must have come across this poor sucker after I got away from them. Looking at his bruises I felt kind of bad. Duke and Preston were both staring at me.

Duke spoke. "Well, kid? We're dealing with an assault here and I can't believe that it had anything to do with a missing kitty. I'm going to need you to tell me all about any other cases you're working on."

This put me in a weird spot. We really didn't have any other cases and I could just tell him that but the state of our business affairs was none of Duke's business. On the other hand, Duke was one of the only creatures in the world that I didn't like to annoy for absolutely no reason. I thought for a couple of seconds and decided if I told him that I wasn't working on anything else he wouldn't believe me anyway so why bother?

"Sorry, Duke" I said, "I got nothing for you."

"C'mon, kid". His tone had somehow slipped from gruff but friendly to just plain gruff. I knew that it was nothing personal but he thought that there was a possibility that I knew something that he didn't and that went against his natural order of things.

"Look, you know me well enough to know that I'm not going to want to answer your question, right?"

Duke stayed silent. He wasn't going to play my game. Preston was more accommodating and answered my question.

"Right."

"Thanks." I continued. "Now knowing that, what would I say if I had another case that would explain the beating that was inflicted on this poor soul?"

"You'd say that you didn't ." said Preston in a matter-of-fact tone of voice.

"Correct! Outright denial. Now, what would I say if I actually had no other cases?"

"You'd also deny it." Preston replied. "Especially if you were a smartaleck little jerk."

"Yeah, especially if I was a – Hey!" Despite Preston's insult, I continued. "Now, I really don't see how you guys expect me to-"

I stopped in mid-sentence. A little Scottie dog was approaching. His name was Rowdy and he was another one of Duke's officers. The snotty one. It was my theory that he was constantly acting like a tough guy to make up for his small stature. He didn't like me because of a move I'd made back when we were all searching for a missing garden gnome and he was the type that held a grudge.

"Hey, boss!" he yelled as he ran up to us. "You gotta come with me! I found –" He stopped abruptly when he saw me.

"What? What is it?" Duke said. He usually wasn't that short with his guys, but he was still annoyed with me.

"Can we talk in private?" Rowdy spoke without taking his eyes off of me. "Let's go over there."

Duke rolled his eyes but agreed. He looked at me and Smoky. "You two stay right here." He Preston and Rowdy went over to the other side of the patio and had a conference in low tones.

Smokey and I stayed in place and tried to listen to what the dogs were discussing. No luck. So I turned to Smokey and said, "I need to talk to you. Where can I find you later?"

He was still hostile. "Look punk, if I felt better I'd love to meet you alone and pay you back for these bruises."

I tried to charm him. "C'mon my friend. I didn't put those bruises on you and I'm sorry you got caught up in whatever is going on. Can't we just have a nice conversation and maybe I can help get the guys that did this to you?"

"Whatever. Why can't we just wait until the dogs leave. They look like they're about to take off."

"Yeah and I'm going to have to follow them. Wherever they're going has something to do with me."

"How do you know that?"

"Well, the little dog isn't that smart." I explained, "You saw how he shut up as soon as he saw me."

"So," Smokey replied, "Maybe its super secret doggie patrol stuff."

"Nah. He saw you and he kept talking. He saw me and he clammed up. They're definitely talking about me."

Smokey didn't say anything so I continued. "If it had been Preston, he wouldn't have stopped talking when he saw me, he would've lied about what he wanted Duke for and told him later when I wasn't around."

"I guess you don't like that little dog."

"You guess right"

"And I guess you like yourself a whole lot."

"I can't help it. I'm a likable kind of cat. It might be contagious. I notice that you've spoken to me twice now without calling me a name. Be that as it may, you and I need to chat."

He rolled his eyes. "I'll be at the tree stump tonight. We can talk there. It looks like the convention is breaking up."

Duke, Preston and Rowdy had stopped talking and were staring at me. "Hey kid." Duke said, "We gotta go. You and me are going to talk later."

"Where are you going?" I asked.

"Dog Patrol business." He answered. "Don't worry about it."

"Can I tag along?" I asked casually. I knew what the likely answer to that was, but they would expect me to ask.

"No need," Duke said. "It's got nothing to do with you."

"Fine. Go ahead, I'll just stay here and have a talk with Smokey." I said in a tone that implied that that was exactly what I wanted to do anyway and that I had somehow tricked them into leaving me alone with Smokey.

"Good." Duke said. "I'll come see you and Yoshi later." He and the other dogs trotted to the driveway on their way to the front of the house.

I counted to ten, gave Smokey a wink and then took off after the dogs.

CHAPTER 3

I followed the dogs for five blocks. They took the sidewalks for the first two blocks until they saw an old man mowing his lawn. If he got a look at three unaccompanied dogs strolling down the sidewalk, he'd probably decide that a call to Animal Control was in order. The only animal control Duke and his boys believed in was the kind that they provided. So they took to travelling through backyards, hopping over and going under fences when necessary. This was ideal for me since there were lots of trees, shrubs and playground equipment for me to duck behind as I trailed the dogs. Duke would occasionally turn and look back to see if anybody was following but he didn't spot me. It was his highly trained police dog eyes against my natural feline stealth. I scored a point for feline stealth as we approached what I assumed was our destination. The last backyard fence that the dogs jumped led to a lot behind an abandoned gas station.

The subdivision that we all lived in was bordered on the east by a major six lane street that was packed with supermarkets, fast food restaurants and gas stations. The street functioned as a sort of a barrier for the neighborhood animals as very few of us were insane enough to try crossing a busy six lane highway. This particular gas station had been closed for awhile. They had opened up a newer sleeker quickie mart across the street and I guess that this spot was going to be abandoned until the humans decided what kind of greasy fast food they wanted to sell from this location. In the meantime there was an empty medium sized building with a garage bay and a couple of raised platforms in front where the gas pumps once stood. The whole lot was paved but there were some weeds popping up through the cracks in the asphalt. While lots of cars were constantly passing by the front of the place, the back was pretty quiet. That was where Duke, Preston and Rowdy had stopped. I hadn't jumped over the last fence, so I was in a backyard looking for a good vantage point. There was a nice big oak tree close to the fence that I could sit behind, hear everything and stick my head out every now again to see what was happening with little chance of the dogs seeing me.

Duke and his boys were about forty feet away from me. I was sure that they wouldn't be able to see me and since the wind was blowing towards me, I was pretty sure that they wouldn't be able to smell me either.

The dogs were just sitting in the middle of the lot waiting for something. They all looked tense. Which I suppose made me tense. Which is probably why I just about jumped out of my skin when a voice from behind me whispered, "Hello".

A lesser cat would've screeched and jumped fifteen feet in the air. Not me. My tail merely puffed up to five or six times its normal size. The voice belonged to Molasses. Of course.

"Did I scare you?" she whispered, seeing the inflated state of my tail.

"Nah, It's a new style. I used the blow dryer on my tail all morning. It's what all the cool kittens are doing." I thought that it would be a good time to change the subject. "What are you doing here?"

"I live around here. I was sitting in the back window and I saw those dogs go through my backyard and then you went by. I thought that you might be working on my problem."

"No, not right now-" I broke off what I was about to say because I saw her eye widen as she saw something going on behind me.

I turned around to see that Duke and company had been joined by three other dogs. It was the pit bulls that Mo and I had encountered last night. I was immediately annoyed with myself for being distracted and not seeing where they had come from. Yoshi was never going to let me hear the end of this.

Things were starting to happen with the dogs. "My name is Duke." Duke announced. "This neighborhood is my jurisdiction. Who are you?"

The leader of the pit bulls smiled. She was in a much better mood than last night. "I don't have time for introductions. Your little punk dog said that you wanted to talk to me. What do you want?"

Molasses whispered to me, "Wow. Aren't they even going to sniff each other?"

"No, they skipped the traditional butt-sniffing greeting. This is as serious as heartworm."

Duke continued, "OK, if that's how you want it. Here's the deal – my guys and I enforce the law around here. My name's Duke. This is Preston and this is Rowdy. Now, if you-"

He was cut off by the obnoxious snickering coming from the pit bulls. Like a good soldier Duke carried on. "We keep this neighborhood nice for the people and animals that live here. So when I hear rumors about dog fighting in a nice place like this, I get interested. You guys know anything about that?"

"Oh, I get it," The leader of the pit bulls said, "You see a bunch of pit bulls and all of sudden, you start asking us about dog fighting. That's discrimination!" Her two friends stood behind her and snickered menacingly.

"What's your name, lady?" Duke growled.

"I'm Nails." She nodded her head towards her two friends. "This is Seven and his name's Nine. And yeah, that's their names not their ages."

Those names started Molasses giggling. I shushed her. She was beautiful but she didn't seem to have a lot of self-control.

"Anything else?" Nails asked Duke.

"Oh, just a few questions. Where do you live? Where do you come from? What's your owner's name? Are you in the neighborhood for a visit or do you think that you're going to be here permanent? What do you know about dogfights? You answer those in order you'd like."

A mean smile was on her scarred lips. "I don't like answering in any order. I don't care about you and your silly doggie scout patrol. I'm not answering anything!"

Nobody said anything for a few seconds. Then Duke spoke. "OK, if that's how you want it. This get together was your idea. Why don't you tell me what it is you want to say?"

"Nothing" She replied. "We heard you were looking for us and I wanted to meet you and get it out of the way. I got nothing to say to you and as far as I'm concerned, you punks have no authority over me and my crew!"

"Listen to me," Duke said, "I'm not impressed by your attitude. If you or anybody with you is doing anything illegal, my boys and I will shut it down. Believe it!"

"Oh please, you and your boys can't even secure a secret meeting. Who's that behind that tree?"

I looked at Molasses. "She's talking about us." I whispered, "Your giggling gave us away."

"It did not!" she said, "It was your shushing. You shush too loud, you giggle shusher!"

"Giggle-shusher! That's the worst kind of shusher! How dare you call me a –"

"Excuse me." Duke's angry voice rang out. "Come out from behind that tree!"

Mo and I stepped out from the tree. All six dogs on the other side of the chain link fence were staring at us. Duke and Rowdy were enraged, Preston rolled his eyes and the pit bulls looked like they wanted to eat us.

"It's those stupid cats from last night!" said Nails. Then she said a word I'd rather not repeat.

"Hey, watch your mouth," I said. "There's a lady present and I ain't talking about you!"

To look at her, you wouldn't think that that was the meanest thing anybody had ever said to her, but she acted like it was. Her scarred face actually looked like her feelings had been hurt for half of a second and then it turned mean again as she turned to the dog called Nine and barked, "Get them!"

Fast as lightning he bolted a couple of steps and then jumped over the fence that separated us from the dogs. Duke and his dogs started to follow him but Nails and Seven jumped in front of them, barking and snapping. That was all I saw of them before my common sense forced me to turn and run. Molasses was a few steps ahead of me and since she knew this area better than I did, I just followed her.

She ran back to the front of the house that we had been behind and made a beeline up the street. She seemed to know where she was going so I decided to trust her and just follow her lead. I just hoped that she wouldn't climb a tree. Nothing is more embarrassing than being chased up a tree. Especially when the Fire Department has to be called to get you down. My heart sank when I saw that she was headed straight for a Douglas Fir. It was very young tree in the middle of a very well maintained front yard. It couldn't have been any taller than five feet and if we climbed it all Nine would have to do is jump moderately high to sink his teeth into us. Following Molasses was starting to seem like a bad idea but at that point, we were all running at full speed and there weren't a lot of other options. Molasses leapt up to the top of the tree. As she was in the air, I finally realized what she was doing. She was brilliant! As she landed on the top, the whole tree bent forward under her weight until she and the treetop were on the ground. The tree strained to get itself upright but Molasses weighed a little too much for it. I had only been a couple steps behind her so I jumped forward, leaping over both Molasses and the bent tree. Nine had been a couple steps behind me and thankfully had only been paying attention to my behind. Seeing me jump, he also jumped forward. With expert timing, Molasses stepped off of the treetop as soon as I had passed over her. It sprang back to its vertical position with enough force and power that it hit Nine right in his face and chest and knocked him into the air. He flipped three times and landed twenty feet away into the hedges of the house next door. Molasses and I kept running and there was no way the he was going to be able to catch up. As we ran we could hear the gradually fading sounds of Nine cussing, yelling and vowing that he was going to get us. We had gone about three blocks before we couldn't hear him anymore. We sat on the sidewalk and panted for a bit, then I looked over at Molasses and said, "I think I'm in love. Every time I see you, my heart beats faster, I get an adrenaline rush and I pant like crazy."

"That's nice," She replied, "But I think I just met a dog that's head over heels in love with me."

As I laughed, she winked at me and trotted home.

CHAPTER 4

I got home at about 1:00. I had checked in with my bird contacts and asked them to keep an eye out for Butterscotch. I desperately needed a nap but I was going to have to report to Yoshi before I could get any sleep. Our humans wouldn't be home until at least 5:30 or maybe 6:00 if I was lucky. Three or four hours of sleep would have to do.

When I walked into the house, I saw Maury the mouse coming through the living room. Maury was an operative that we used when the workload required more than just me. Yoshi must have called him in.

"Hey Maury," I said as I repressed a desire to attack and eat him.

"G-Gatsby! How are you?" He squeaked nervously. I assumed that the nervousness had to do with the fact that he knew that I was suppressing a desire to attack and eat him. I get that a lot from mice and birds.

"So what's going on? You get a job from Yoshi?"

"Yep." He said, "I'm just coming from meeting with him."

"What's he got you doing?"

I knew what he was going to say before he did. If Yoshi had called him in without telling me, it was for something that I wasn't supposed to know about.

"Uh, I'm really sorry but he gave me strict instructions not to tell anybody anything. Sorry." It looked like he was genuinely pained to tell me this.

"I don't think that would include me, his partner."

Maury gulped. "Um. Especially you. I'm sorry."

Maury was afraid of me but he still wasn't going to tell me what was going on. Continuing the conversation was pointless.

"Whatever." I dismissed him and trotted off towards the stairs. He sighed and then went off on his top-secret mission.

I found Yoshi in the home office. He was reading. Our man had a variety of different kinds of books on a couple of seven foot tall bookshelves and Yoshi would help himself. He knew how to read and would knock books off of the bookshelf during the afternoon. The people assumed that the books fell off when we were climbing up the shelves. Today Yoshi was reading something about the Civil War. Fascinating.

"I'm back." I announced.

He lifted the whiskers over his left eye. "You've been gone for three hours. That must have been some conversation."

"It was more than conversation; I've had a very eventful morning." I said. "Do I report now or can I get some sleep?"

Yoshi considered this. He had his faults but he genuinely hated to keep any cat from sleep. Although he didn't hate it that much because his next words were: "I think it would be better if you reported now. You'll have time for a nap."

So I told Yoshi everything that had happened since I'd left that morning. He sat on his haunches and listened without interrupting. When I had finished I let loose with a huge yawn, just to emphasize the point that some cats hadn't been in bed all morning.

It didn't matter. He had comments and questions. His first question was one that I had been hoping that he would skip.

"Which direction did the pit bulls come from?"

I cleared my throat then answered, "I believe that I mentioned that I didn't see where they came from. I was speaking with our client."

He rolled his eyes, which is a good trick for a cat. If you don't believe me ask your cat. Just asking that question will probably make him try but odds are that he won't be able to do it.

"So you were too preoccupied by this girl to observe vital information?"

"Oh, come on!" I protested. "I knew that you wouldn't be happy but aren't you overdoing it? How is that vital information?"

He looked at me like someone who is being very patient with a very slow child. "Duke suspects that these dogs are involved with dog fighting, doesn't he?"

"Yeah, from the way they look you don't have to be Sherlock Holmes to make that deduction. What does that have to do with a missing cat?" As those words were coming out of my mouth, I suddenly realized what he was getting at. "Oh!"

A couple of months ago Yoshi had told me stories about dogfighting and how it was controlled by vicious, nasty people who had no regard for animal life. There were stories about housepets being kidnapped and forced to fight dogs either as a training method for the pit bulls or to make the dogs more bloodthirsty. Yoshi had told me about this in an effort to get me to be more careful when I went outside the house.

I usually ignore stories like this because Yoshi was full of horrible stories of the bad things that humans do to animals. Usually at this time of the year, he would go on and on about his belief that every Halloween, devil worshipping teenagers would abduct black cats and hurt them while trying to practice witchcraft. I get around a lot and I read the newspaper but I've never actually heard of anything like this happening. When I try to tell that to Yoshi, he just sniffs and talks about how everybody hates black cats and cover-up the crimes committed against them. For most of October not only will he not go outside but he'll stay away from windows at nights and weekends for fear that some crazed teenager will see him and abduct him to use in some weird ritual.

So I'd never known how seriously to take his "pets being kidnapped to be sparring partners for pit bulls" story. Maybe as serious as a case of heartworm.

"So you think that he got kidnapped and is being used to train dogfighters?" I asked.

"I don't know. But if we can find out where these dogs are living, we can determine whether or not Butterscotch is there. At the least, we can have Duke shut them down. The thought that there might be dogfights going on in this neighborhood sickens me."

I considered that for a minute. "So is that what I'm supposed to do tonight? Track those dogs down?"

"Yes, talk with the cats that live in the area around that gas station."

"Got it. Anything else?" There was always something else.

"Yes. Have Molasses here at 11:30 tomorrow morning. Assuming she can tell time."

"Really?"

"Yes, I have a few questions that I'd like to ask her myself. I also want to meet the woman who has you in such a state that you can't even tell me a simple thing like from which direction a pack of vicious dogs came from."

This would have been an ideal time to roll my eyes if I could. I couldn't so I just asked if there was anything else.

"I also would like to talk to that other cat, Smoky. Please arrange for him to come here tomorrow at about noon. That's all. Go get some sleep."

"On my way," I said, "But I have one question for you. I saw Maury leaving. Is he doing anything that I need to know about?"

"No." That was all he said. He had gone back to his book.

"Well if that's how it's going to be, fine. I'm going to sleep." I turned around and trotted to the sweet bliss of the living room couch.

"One more thing." He stopped me in my tracks just as I'd reached the doorway.

"What?" I said.

"Did you find out what Percy wanted?"

"Nope. He was locked in his house when I went by this morning. Maybe I'll see him tonight."

Yoshi shook his head. "Your priority tonight is finding out where those dogs live. Percy will wait."

"You got it." I said. Then I yawned and headed off to dreamland.

CHAPTER 5

I'm going to skip ahead to the next day. The previous night I had arranged with Molasses to be at our house at 11:30. Then I had seen Smoky and he'd promised to show up at noon, although he still had a very nasty attitude. I had gotten nowhere asking the neighborhood cats if they knew anything about the pit bulls or dogfights. Cats are usually keen observers of everything, especially things involving dogs but in this case no cat seemed to know anything.

So it was 11:30 on Halloween morning and Yoshi was perched on the kitchen windowsill waiting for our appointment with Molasses. I was outside, sitting in the grass about six feet away from the window. The weather was ok for late October, with grey skies and only a slight chill in the air. The human children should be able to trick or treat tonight without having to wear coats over their costumes.

At 11:35 Molasses appeared. She walked up and sat down beside me. Yoshi looked down on us from the bay window.

I did the introductions. "Molasses, this is Yoshi. Yoshi, Molasses."

"Hi." She said.

"Hello." He replied. "Unfortunately I don't have any news of your brother. I had a couple of questions that I wanted to ask you directly."

She smiled. "Shoot."

Yoshi started with standard questions that went over stuff that I had already covered with her. Did Butterscotch have any enemies? Was he likely to run away? He asked a bunch of other questions that made me think that this was a waste of time. Then he asked something that I thought was completely from out of left field: "Is your brother a participant in cat shows?"

I thought that he'd run out of questions and was just fishing around but she answered in the affirmative. "Yes," she said

"He's a show cat. He's great too. He's taken first place in his breed at the last three shows he's competed in."

Yoshi stopped to consider this information. I jumped in with my own question. "Are there any shows coming up?"

"Sure, there's one next week at the convention center."

I followed up. "Do you think that his disappearance might have anything to do with the cat show?"

She laughed. "Do you mean that he got stage fright and ran away? No, he's a very confident cat. He always assumes that he's going to win. He wouldn't run off because of that."

Yoshi spoke up. "I don't think that's what Gatsby had in mind. He was probably thinking of something more sinister. Does Butterscotch have any rivals at the cat shows?"

"Rivals, you mean like enemies?" She said as if she were shocked by the question. "I think that you guys have the wrong impression of cat shows. It's a great atmosphere. We're all friends."

I could tell by the look on his face that Yoshi wasn't buying that. "I'm sorry. I admit that I don't know a lot about cat shows but my knowledge of feline nature makes me believe that a cat show would be a hotbed of treachery and backstabbing."

Molasses smiled at him. "I like the way you talk." she said, "I'm not sure that you're saying much but it sounds good. What do you mean by feline nature?"

"We cats are part of a species that include the animal kingdom's most perfect hunters, the world's most brutally efficient fighters and most of us are shrewd, resourceful and sharp-witted. With all of these gifts it's not surprising that we can also be a little arrogant, self-righteous and stubborn. Especially towards each other. I find it unbelievable that these strong inborn characteristics don't emerge during a competition."

She thought about that for a moment and then said, "Is that what you guys tell yourselves to get through the day? That you're really panthers and lions? You may not have heard, but housecats have been domesticated for thousands of years. As far

as I'm concerned we are warm, friendly and completely loveable.
"

Apparently Yoshi didn't feel like arguing. "Whatever. Can you tell Gatsby the names and homes of Butterscotch's rivals at the cat show?"

The smile came back to her face. "Sure, but we'd have to start with me."

"Is that so?"

"Yes, I've come in second to him in the last four shows we've been in."

"How did you feel about that?" Yoshi asked.

"I wasn't happy about it. But I haven't done away with him or anything"

"Did your owners treat you any differently since he was always the winner?"

She snorted. "No, if anything they spent more time with me, trying to get me over the hump."

"Could he have run away, thinking that you were going to beat him?"

"No. Absolutely not. He goes into these shows believing without a doubt that he's the best cat. He's not the type that feels threatened."

"Is there anyone else that he might consider a threat?" Yoshi asked.

"No. There are other cats that compete with us, but he wouldn't consider them threats. He thinks very highly of himself."

"I suppose so. I'd still like you to tell Gatsby about any other rival cats in these shows. Now, I have an appointment in a few minutes. Do you have any questions for me?"

"Actually I do. I have a question for you and your uncharacteristically quiet friend here." She nodded in my direction. I returned the nod and she continued. "Gatsby hasn't mentioned anything about payment. And the other pets that I talked to about you guys said that you didn't charge for your services. Is that right?"

"Mostly." Yoshi said. "Although we've been known to keep a portion if we recover something delicious. We mostly work pro bono"

She looked puzzled. "For bones? That sounds more like what a dog would charge."

No. Pro Bono is a latin term. It means gratis-," he stopped himself and started over. "It means for free. We mostly work for free."

"Why? What's in it for you?"

I could tell from the look on Yoshi's face that, despite what he had just said about having an appointment in a few minutes, we were in for a speech.

"Well let's go back to what I said about feline nature. Gatsby and I are hunters by nature but the life of a housecat provides very little in the way of prey. Our needs for food and shelter are satisfied but at the expense of our instinctual need to hunt. This could result in boredom. So to fight our boredom, we try to solve problems for the pets in our neighborhood."

At that point I felt the need to speak up. "Of course one of us can only heed our hunting instincts when they're not during our regularly scheduled naptimes or mealtimes or if we're not reading or if we never have to leave the house or do anything that might make us uncomfortable -"

"That's enough." Yoshi hissed. "What happened to you being uncharacteristically quiet?"

I just grinned at him so he turned to Molasses and said, "Miss Molasses, I'm afraid that I have another meeting. If you don't mind, Gatsby will escort you to the front of the house and I'm sure you can find your way home from there."

"Can't he walk me home?"

I tried to look apologetic. "Sorry kid, I'm needed here." As we walked to the front of the house I was able to get a few names and addresses of Butterscotch's rivals at the cat shows. I told her that I would have loved to walk her home but duty called. I watched her walk away until she was a couple blocks away. Then I went back to Yoshi.

Smokey was already there, sitting in the spot that I had vacated. He didn't look much better than he had the last time I'd seen him and the grimace on his face indicated that his attitude wasn't any better either. He and Yoshi were already talking but something else grabbed my attention. I had glanced over my shoulder and noticed a tiny grey shape dart across our driveway and into the hedges. I was pretty sure that it Maury the mouse. The most likely reason that he would be out at this time of day is whatever secret mission he was doing for Yoshi. Was he following Molasses? Was he watching to see if someone else had been following Molasses? Was he looking out to warn us in case the pit bulls showed up? I didn't know the answers to any of those questions so I just sat down and told Smokey a lie.

"You're looking better."' I said.

"Shut up!" He replied, friendly as ever.

Yoshi ignored Smokey's rudeness. "Smokey and I had just introduced ourselves. I was just telling him that he should really see a vet."

"Wow," I said, "You wouldn't tell your worst enemy to go to the vet."

Smokey growled, "The only way I'm going to a vet is if Animal Control snatches me. No thanks. I'll heal up fine eventually."

"Ah yes, the rigors of being a stray."

"How would a punk like you know, in your fancy house?"

Yoshi sighed. "I was on the streets for a few months in my youth. In some ways it was the best time of my life. If you envy my comfort, I envy your independence. Whatever!" He waved that topic away. "I called you here to ask you about the attack you suffered the other day. Can you tell me what happened?"

Smokey glared at me, apparently thinking that I hadn't told Yoshi what I had learned yesterday. Before I could open my mouth to defend myself, he spoke. "Well, I was over on Colston drive when those three pit bulls came at me."

"What was the nearest intersection?"

"What?"

"I'd like to know exactly where this took place."

"OK, it was two houses down from McKinley. Anyway, these dogs come from out of nowhere and had me surrounded!"

Yoshi looked impatient, "What do you mean 'from out of nowhere'? Which direction did they come from?"

"I don't know!" Smokey's usual enraged attitude had abated for a second and he seemed a little flustered. "It happened fast. I just looked up and they were all around me."

Yoshi didn't seem convinced of this. "You must be one incredibly self absorbed cat to not notice three pit bulls coming at you. Can you at least tell me if they all came from the same direction or from three different directions?"

"I don't know. What are you, an idiot? They were together; wouldn't they have all had to have come from the same direction?"

Yoshi sighed. "I suppose so. Then what happened?"

"The girl one told me to relax, that they weren't going to hurt me."

"Is that exactly what she said?"

"Yeah, but I didn't have my secretary there taking notes so who can be sure?"

Yoshi sighed again. "There's no need for sarcasm. I just want everything as factual as possible."

"Fine. That's what she said."

"What happened next?"

"Then she asked me if I knew a cat named Gatsby. I said no and she goes, 'Stop lying, all of you cats know each other. When you see Gatsby, tell him to mind his own business.' Then they gave me a beatdown." He looked at me. "So I figure I owe this jerk a beating."

I said, "You come look me up when your boo-boos are all better."

Yoshi spoke up. "I wouldn't recommend it. Gatsby may be smaller than you but he's quite a roughneck. Your issue seems to be more with these pit bulldogs than with him. Is there anything you can tell us that would help find them?"

"No. And I don't see what you could do about it anyway. You or that German Shepherd that thinks he's a cop."

"Maybe not. Let me ask you this: We have reason to believe that the dogs that attacked you are involved in dogfighting. Do you know anything about that?"

The question seemed to startle Smokey. He hesitated for a second, then answered. "What? They didn't say anything about dogfighting. I don't know anything about that."

DING! DING! DING! The lie detector in my head was going off. Yoshi's question had caught him off guard and his angry facade dropped for a minute. I didn't quite get how he could have had anything to do with a dogfighting ring but the way his attitude shifted from confusion to innocence to denial made me sure that he was lying.

If Yoshi agreed he wasn't showing it. "Fine. I believe I'm done. You don't have any questions, do you Gatsby?" His tone made it pretty clear that I'd better not. "Have a nice rest of your day."

Smokey looked up at Yoshi, then at me then back at Yoshi. He still seemed a little on edge from the dogfighting question but the anger was back. "Well that was a whole lot of nothing. Thanks for wasting my time!" With that Mr. Personality turned and trotted off towards the back of the house.

I must have been in a strange pose because Yoshi asked me. "What are you thinking of doing?"

I looked up at him. "I'm going to wait a couple of seconds and then follow him. Maybe we can salvage something out of dragging him here."

"No," Yoshi said, "That won't be necessary."

"What! How could it not be necessary? You know as well as I do that he was lying about not knowing anything about the dogfighting."

"Oh yes. But he knows you. If you try following him, he'll probably spot you."

I snorted. "Oh please. Nobody spots me."

"I'm well aware of your abilities, but why take chances? Why don't you go take a nap?"

"Look I'm a cat of action. Unlike you, I only need four or five naps a day."

"Ah, to be young and annoying." Yoshi answered, and then he let loose with a massive yawn. "You're four years old. When you're nine like me, you'll appreciate the importance of rest. Since you have so much energy, why don't you go see what Percy wants?"

"What?"

"Percy the bulldog? Remember him?"

"Yeah I remember him. I thought we were going to blow him off."

"Apparently you need something to do while we're awaiting developments on our other cases."

I smirked. "Does 'awaiting developments' mean that you don't know what to do next?"

"No. It means go see Percy and leave me alone." He turned so he could jump down from the windowsill and presumably go off to another nap.

"Hold on!" I said, "I've got a question to further my education in whatever it is that we do."

Yoshi sighed at having to put off his rest for another thirty seconds. "What is it?"

"Why did you ask Molasses about cat shows? I mean, that came out of nowhere but it was dead-on."

Yoshi sighed again. "It wasn't from out of nowhere. You need to pay more attention. You told me that Molasses had described her brother as having a thirty point face, didn't you?"

"Yes."

"That's not generally a common way to describe a cat. That's cat show talk. I'll see you when I wake up." With that he turned around and jumped down. I could hear him go "thump" on the kitchen floor and trot off to bed. I starting walking towards

Percy's house wondering how in the world I was supposed to

know how people talked at cat shows.

CHAPTER 6

I didn't go straight to Percy's. It had occurred to me that a nap might not be such a bad idea, so it wasn't until late afternoon that I set off to Percy's house. I didn't sleep that well as I spent a lot of time wondering why Yoshi hadn't let me follow Smokey. He obviously knew something about the dogfighting. Even though our main objective was finding Butterscotch, if we could get information on the dog fighting and shut it down, why not? Something about Smokey had annoyed me from the first time I met him. He didn't seem like any stray cat I had ever met. His coarse language was okay but his haughty attitude just seemed wrong. He always acted like he was the most important cat in the room, which isn't something that you would expect from a stray. Then there was his attitude towards me. He really didn't seem to like me at all. There really had to be something seriously wrong with him.

The good thing about Percy is that at this time of day you always knew where to find him. Late afternoon would find him chained in the backyard. The other good thing about Percy is that he was usually chained. His bark may be worse than his bite but who needs to test that theory?

I found him in his backyard, furiously barking at a toad. The toad was just beyond the reach of Percy's chain and was just sitting in the grass, unimpressed by Percy's histrionics.

"Yo, Percival!" I called. "What's up? You busy keeping dangerous prowlers at bay?"

"Well it's about time." he responded. Then he looked around. "Where's your boss?"

"Yoshi has better things to do. I wish I did. What do you want?"

"Well it's too late now!"

"Too late for what?" I impulsively responded. I instantly regretted having said that. I could've just accepted that I was too late and turned around and left. Nope, I had to ask.

"Too late to get me trained for the dogfights!"

Never mind what I just said about regretting my question. "What are you talking about?"

"I heard that there was going to be dog fights going down in the neighborhood tonight and we all know that I'm top dog around here! I —"

I had to interrupt. He would go on like that forever. "OK, so what does this have to do with Yoshi and me?"

"I wanted Yoshi to train me and be my manager!"

I would've laughed my tail off if I wasn't so keyed up that Percy might have some info on the dog fighting ring. Ever since we had chased away a giant rat that had been bullying him, Percy had gotten the idea that there was nothing that Yoshi couldn't do. I decided to try some logic.

"Don't humans run this dogfighting thing?"

"Yeah!"

"Do you actually you think that your owner's going to take you and put you in a fight?"

"What?" He thought about this for a minute. "Naw, he's too lame. We'll have to go by ourselves."

"I don't pretend to know how this stuff works, but you really think that they'll let you fight without an owner?"

"Uh, I don't know. They'll see how awesome I am and they'll have to put me in!"

"Then what?" I asked.

"Then I'm going to beat down some fool and make some money!"

"Do you think that the humans running this are going to give a dog money?"

He knew that I was getting at something but he wasn't getting it. Then a light seemed to go on in his empty head. "Oh, I get it." He said. "If Yoshi's my manager, I guess they would pay him. Talent like me shouldn't be handling the money."

I took a deep breath and let out a long deep cat sigh. "Look there's three things wrong with your plan. Number one is that nobody knows where these dog fights are so we wouldn't be able to –"

"I know where they are!" He said indignantly.

"What? How?"

"Same way I found out about them in the first place. This ugly girl and her two buddies were cutting through my yard the other night so I told them to get moving. You know the routine. They laughed at me 'cause I was tied down with this stupid chain." He grimaced. "They told me if I was really tough that I'd be at the dog fights on Halloween and settle with them then."

I was getting impatient. "OK, so where is it?"

"They're in that abandoned brick house off of Sunbury." His eyes narrowed. "Now are you guys going to help me or not?"

"No. For two reasons now. Reason number one is that you would get torn to shreds. Not that that would be so horrible but I don't want to have anything to do with it. Reason number two is that the humans who run this sick stuff are not going to let a dog enter by himself and if you win they're certainly not going to give you any money! These people exploit animals for profit and the only thing they're giving dogs is pain and misery!"

He looked at me with hard eyes and growled, "You better watch your tone, cat. Don't talk to me like I'm stupid. One of these days I'm not going to be chained to this house."

Which was a good point, but I couldn't resist asking him a question: "And how in the world were you planning to spend money? Were you going to walk into a store with a wad of cash in your mouth, go to the meat counter and ask for prime rib?"

He just glared at me. I walked away wondering what exactly he thought he was going to do with money.

CHAPTER 7

I took off immediately in the direction of the brick house that Percy had mentioned. I knew exactly where it was and it would only take ten minutes to get there. As I walked I tried to figure out what I was going to do when I got there. I wanted to make sure that it was the place where the dogfights were being held and if so, I wanted to see if they had Butterscotch and if so, I wanted to rescue him and take him to Molasses. That was a whole lot of "if so's". Anyway if I could tell for sure that the dogfights were operating out of that house, I could tell Duke and he could get his owner and the human police to shut them down. If you're out there reading this and you think that I should've went straight to Duke first, you're probably correct but that's not the way I do things.

On the south end of our subdivision, the backyards extended into woods. On the other side of these woods was a hill and on top of the hill was an old two story brick house that was at least a hundred and fifty years old. The house hadn't been lived in for a long time and looked awful. The windows had all been broken by rowdy children and the white paint on the windowframes and pillars was flaking. In spite of all this, the house still gave off a homey vibe. I had made it through the woods and was sitting behind a tree looking up at the house. I thought that I could hear barking. I decided to stop and think. If anybody was in the house looking out of a window, they might see me coming. The smart thing to do would be to leave and come back after dark. That way I could let Yoshi know what I'd found out and see if he had any ideas. He really hadn't contributed much to this affair so far.

At this point I was used to Molasses sneaking up behind me so I didn't react at all when she walked up behind me. In fact before she could say anything, I said, "What's new, pussycat? What are you doing here?"

"You passed by my house and you were moving fast. I thought maybe you had a lead on my brother, so I followed you."

Great. To get from Percy's to the brick house, I did have to pass through Molasses' neighborhood and I was so preoccupied that she must have followed me through the woods without me noticing. If Yoshi ever found out, here's another thing that I'd never hear the end of.

"So is Butterscotch in there?" she asked.

"I sure hope not." I replied. "I think that that's where they're having dogfights."

She shuddered. "Ew! That's gross!" The she gave me doubtful look. "I haven't heard of any dogfights around here. Are you sure?"

"Well my source of information is unreliable to say the least." I admitted. "But I see two cars and a truck in the driveway of a house that has been abandoned for as long as I've lived here."

She looked at the cars and the pickup truck that I had indicated. "That's probably people renovating the house."

"Could be."

"Do you think that Butterscotch is in there?" She asked.

"Is he good at interior design?"

"No smart guy, I mean that if that is in fact a house where they have dogfights do you think that Butterscotch is in there?"

"I don't know." I admitted.

"So what are you going to do?"

"I'm going to watch the house until I know what's going on. We call that surveillance."

"Good plan," she said. Then she started walking up the hill. "I don't have enough patience for surveillance. I'm going to go look in the windows." She said over her shoulder.

I ran after her. "Wait up. That's what I was going to do anyway. I just thought that you might be impressed with me if I used a big word like 'surveillance'."

We went around the hill so that we could approach the house from the windowless eastern side. Hopefully no windows meant that no one would see us coming.

Despite the vehicles in the driveway, the house still seemed deserted. The most prominent sound that we could hear was the leaves rustling as they blew over the grass but I was sure that I could hear a lot of angry barking coming from inside the house.

We had just gotten right up against the house when Mo commented, "Wow. A spooky old house. All we need is a black cat to make Halloween complete. So where's your buddy?"

"Keep your voice down," I whispered. "Yoshi wouldn't be caught dead outside of the house on Halloween. Well any night really, but especially Halloween."

We sat looked, listened and smelled for a few minutes but we weren't gaining any new information. "Wait here," I said. "I'm going to check things out."

I wasn't gone long. I just went around the house, searching for any clues as to what was going on inside.

"Well?" Mo asked when I got back.

"There are definitely dogs in there."

I could smell that from down the hill. Anything else?"

"There's a barrel in the back. It collects water from the busted gutter for some reason. It's pretty full from that storm a couple of nights ago" I said.

She gave me a look.

"Nothing else." I admitted.

"Let's go in!" she said. She really was impatient. She walked over towards the front of the house and I followed.

"What? Do you want to get torn to shreds?"

"I want to find Butterscotch. How else are we going to know if he's in there?"

I tried to be a voice of reason. "We can stop and think of a way that doesn't involve certain death."

She stopped and looked up at a busted first floor window. "I'm going in that window. I know you're not a coward so let's go!"

I wasn't so sure of that but I wasn't going to let her know so we were going inside. I figured that our chances of getting back out were low but I wasn't going to have her think that I was a coward.

"OK then." I said. Oh boy.

The window that she's been talking about had a huge hole in the glass, probably made by some rock throwing boy. It was an easy way for us to gain entry to the house. As she crouched down to jump up to the windowsill, I tried one last attempt to be logical. "This is incredibly dangerous. I know that you're worried about your brother and that blood's thicker than water but –"

She stopped and looked at me. "Butterscotch and I aren't blood relatives. We've just lived together since we were kittens."

"You're roommates?"

"Well, we're good friends."

I didn't like the sound of that. I admit that I may have been feeling a little jealous. "How good?" I asked.

"Not as good as he wanted." She said as she got ready to jump.

"What does that mean?"

She sighed. "He's wanted to get romantic for years but I just think of him as my brother. Is now really a good time for this discussion? I'm going in!" With that she jumped up to the windowsill.

That had gone about as well as any other time that I had tried to be the voice of reason. I jumped up beside her and then we went through the broken window into the dark old house.

We seemed to be in the living room. Although the air was heavy with the smell of dog and we could hear them barking, there were no dogs to be seen. Also no people, no furniture and no light. The only light source in the room was the fading sunlight coming in through the window we'd just entered. I heard some human voices upstairs and some barking coming from downstairs and both sets of voices sounded vicious. I didn't like being here. I looked at Mo. Her eyes glowed a little in the darkness.

"Where would he be?" She whispered.

"I don't know." I answered, "The animal activity seems to be coming from downstairs."

There was a stairway leading down directly across from our window. She nodded in that direction. Since we had smelled the scent of enraged pit bull since we had entered that house but hadn't seen one, it was safe to assume that the dogs were restrained. Regardless it was still a stupid idea to go down those stairs. But I went anyway and Molasses was close behind.

At the sixth step down I could see into the room into which we were descending. It was a pretty big unfinished basement with the floor and walls made of concrete. It suddenly got cold, as if the temperature had dropped twenty degrees. In the middle of the room was a crude ring with a diameter of about eight feet. It was surrounded by a three foot high wall. The room was empty except for a bunch of folding chairs stacked against a wall. "This must be where the magic's going to happen." I whispered as we reached the bottom of the stairway.

Molasses didn't respond. She was staring at the open doorway on the other side of the room. It was the source of the barking that we'd heard upstairs. I didn't hear or smell any humans in there. She looked at me. I nodded. We crept towards the doorway, keeping low and moving along the walls. When we got to the doorway we stopped and poked our heads into the next room. Molasses gasped at what we saw.

It was a much smaller room, longer but a lot more narrow than the room we were coming from and on one side of it was about a dozen cages built from two by fours and chicken wire. The cages were stacked on top of one another, so that there were three rows containing four cages. There was a pit bull inside each cage and none of them looked happy about their present situation. They looked hungry and mean with glowing red eyes glaring out from their hard, scarred faces.

There were a few more cages lined up against the wall at the far end of the room that we couldn't see from the doorway. We were going to have to fully enter the room to see if one of those cages contained Molasses's brother (or friend, or whatever). We'd come this far so there didn't seem to be any point in hesitating now. I walked into the room as casually as I could, looked up at the cages and said, "What's up, dogs?"

The room went insane. The dogs unleashed a torrent of mean, nasty barks and growls. They rammed themselves into the chicken wire but fortunately the cages were much sturdier than they looked. Ignoring the dogs, I walked past the first section of cages so that I could see into the next section. Molasses followed close behind me, anxious to get a look. These cages were empty.

Molasses breathed a sigh of relief. "I want to find him." She said, "But not in here."

I said, "Good, now that we know for sure that he's not in here, can we leave?"

She was looking up. "What's that?"

I saw that she was staring at a round hole in the wall. It was a foot wide and about eight feet off the ground. "I think it's a laundry chute."

"A what?"

"The humans put their dirty clothes in it and they drop down here, where the washer and dryer would be. Then they don't have to carry a heavy basket down the stairs."

"Really?" She kept looking at it.

"Look, Butterscotch is not in there." I said. I was getting very impatient. "Now let's go before something bad happens."

"The only way you're leaving here is in little bits and pieces." said the last voice in the world that I wanted to hear at that particular moment.

"Hi, Nails!" I said, "You're looking good!" I was lying. She looked as hideous as ever. She stood in the doorway with her two henchmen on either side. Nine was glaring at me with ferocity, I imagine that he was replaying our previous encounter in his head and thinking that he was about to get his revenge.

He was probably right. They were blocking the only way out of the room and I really didn't think that I was going to be able to fight the three of them. The best I could hope for was to keep them busy long enough for Molasses to escape. Whatever was about to happen, I probably wasn't going to leave this room.

I took a step towards them to make sure that I was between them and Molasses.

"Look guys, we don't want any trouble!" I said. Then I whispered to Molasses, "I'll try to keep them busy. You get ready to run!"

"Are you a complete idiot?" she hissed. "Just follow me!"

Quick as lightning she spun around and jumped up at the empty cages that were behind us. She bounced off of the cages and propelled herself right into the laundry chute hole. Nails and her henchdogs were taken aback by this for a couple of seconds but then Nails recovered nodded her head in my direction and snarled "Well, get him!"

It didn't seem like a good idea to wait for them so I spun around and made the same jumps that Molasses had made. As I made the first leap towards the cages, I could feel one of the dogs teeth snapping shut just millimeters away from my tail. But they couldn't reach me and I ended up sitting next to Molasses in the laundry chute hole. I smiled at her. "Hey, Beautiful!"

The hole that we had jumped into had a very small ledge that we were sitting in and then went back into a very steep diagonal aluminum surface for about half a foot and then it was a completely vertical shaft going up to the first floor. It was pretty much a big metal tube that was way too steep for even a cat to climb. Obviously people would drop their dirty clothes into the metal shaft and they would fall down the chute and land on the basement floor. Why they just didn't throw the clothes down the stairs was anybody's guess. It was a simple domestic convenience that was now saving me and Molasses's lives.

Nails walked up to the wall until she was directly beneath us. "You can't stay up there forever."

"Oh, I don't see why not." I answered. "It's not too snug of a fit and the company is certainly nice." I winked at Molasses who was looking a little nervous.

Nails on the other hand was suddenly looking very smug. That was not a good thing. "Hey Nine!" she called, "You busy?"

He trotted up to her. "Naw, Boss. What do you need?"

"How would you like to go upstairs and take a ride down the laundry chute?"

Nine's scarred face broke into a big smile. "After the way they made a fool out of me yesterday? I would love to."

"What's going to happen?" Molasses whispered.

"Nine is going to drop down the laundry chute." I replied. "When he hits the bottom of the chute, he'll knock us right into the waiting fangs and claws of Nails and Seven" I looked at Nails. "Is that the plan?"

"You got it." She snarled. "Nobody said that you weren't smart. Just not smart enough."

Nine laughed and said "I'll be right back!" He happily trotted out of the room.

It was a bad situation. All of the dogs in the cages were going nuts, barking and growling all kinds of rude things. Nails was waiting on the concrete floor directly beneath me, looking up at us and working her mouth in practice chomps, giving Molasses and me a preview of what she was going to do to us. Seven sat next to her, quiet but still menacing. It suddenly occurred to me that I had never heard Seven speak. Could he speak? Had he suffered some injury that had rendered him unable to utter a sound?

Then I realized that Molasses wasn't as nervous anymore. Sitting so close to her, I could tell that for some reason she had calmed slightly down. Given our current situation, that made no sense. Had she noticed something that could get us out of this mess? I certainly wasn't seeing anything in the room that would have a calming effect. Was she hearing something comforting? I listened up. I had already been hearing the caged dogs barking insanely and the sound of Nine climbing the stairs. Was there anything else? Yes! I could hear car doors slamming outside. A bunch of cars and SUVs were now outside the house, I had been too preoccupied to hear them driving up and parking but Molasses must have heard them. Next I could hear at least eight men approaching the front of the house while three were going towards the back. There were also four dogs out there. For all I knew, these were more bad humans with dogs for the dogfights that were going to happen tonight. Whoever they were, I might be able to use the interruption to find some way to escape.

I was thinking about this when I heard somebody outside yell, "Open up! It's the police!"

That caused all kinds of frenzied activity in the humans on the second floor. Whatever they were doing didn't matter as a couple of seconds later the front and back doors were busted open and the cops and dogs stormed into the house.

Taking a chance, I yelled, "Hey Duke! We're in the basement!"

I could hear dogs bolt for the basement and a man yelling, "Hey, Duke! Come back, boy!"

Nails and Seven also heard what was going on and they were not happy. Seven had turned to stare at the door to see who was about to come in while Nails just kept glaring at us with pure hate.

Four dogs burst into the room. Duke, Rowdy and two actual official K-9 corps dogs that I didn't know. The caged dogs took the barking up a notch but nobody cared. Nails had turned to face the doorway as she and Seven crouched into a fighting stance and emitted low, steady growls.

One of the K-9 corps dogs stepped forward and said, "Stand down, you two. You're under arrest."

I would've guessed that Nails would be the type of dog that would resist arrest and I would be correct. Nails jumped at the cop dog as soon as he had stepped into range. It didn't matter as Duke had pounced up and was on her before she could do any damage. He clamped his jaws around her neck, plucking her out of mid-air. Then he jerked his head and released his grip, flinging her into the nearest wall. She smashed hard into the cinderblock wall, slid to the floor and stayed there. Seven didn't move. He stayed in his fighting stance but he wasn't moving a muscle. I didn't know what had happened to Nine, but he obviously was no longer a threat. Molasses had fully relaxed and rubbed against me. Footsteps were coming down the stairway in the next room and the two cop dogs trotted off to meet their masters, leaving Duke and Rowdy to guard the prisoners. Rowdy was looking pretty shocked as he stared at the crazed dogs in the cages. Duke just maintained a professional attitude as he kept watch over Nails and Seven.

When he looked up at Molasses and me, I gave him a wink.

"Hey Duke!" I said, "I think I might have some information about those dogfights you were talking about the other day."

CHAPTER 8

Duke managed to sneak Molasses and me out of the house, past the police and animal control officers that were all over the place. All of the cops seemed pretty horrified at what had been going on in that house. The human criminals had all been arrested and taken away and I had never even gotten a look at them. Nails, Seven, Nine and all of the other dogs had been taken by animal control and put in vans. Nails screamed on the way out about all of the terrible things that she was going to do to me.

Duke led us out of the house and to the backyard where we sat in the grass right behind the house. Night had fallen, but there was still plenty of light from the big fat moon overhead. If that wasn't enough, the trees were showing the flashing red and blue lights pulsing from the cop cars up front. Duke sat down in the grass, facing the back of the house. Molasses and I sat facing him, with our backs to the house. I was right next to the big wooden barrel that caught the runoff rain from the roof. I could sense that the barrel was full of water but I figured that none of it would spill on us.

I looked at Duke. "Excellent timing, Duke my man. How did you find us?"

"I got a tip!" He growled angrily.

That seemed odd. He should have been happy about getting a tip like that. He was probably a hero. Why would he be mad? There was only one reason I could think of. "From Yoshi?" I asked.

"Yes!" hissed a voice. I almost jumped out of my skin when Yoshi walked out from around the corner of the house.

I don't want to overstate how shocked and surprised I was to see Yoshi there but in the years that I had known him, he had only gone outside for trips to the vet and even then under extreme and violent protest. To see him out and about on Halloween night was the last thing that I would have ever expected to see. He looked fine, only someone who knew him as well as me could have seen how furious he was.

Duke's mood seemed to lighten. "I've known Yoshi since he was a kitten and I've never seen him as scared as when he came to tell me where you were."

That puzzled me. "How did he know where I was?"

Yoshi spoke up. "Well, it certainly wasn't from you, now was it? When a situation like this arises, you have been trained to report to me before you take any action!"

Duke snorted. "Like that would have done any good!" He looked at me. "Look kid, from what I saw in there you came real close to going to the big litter box in the sky. You knew that all you had to do was call me and I could've gotten the Sheriff to raid the place. Why would you do something so incredibly stupid as going in there by yourself?"

I didn't have anything to say. My mind was so occupied with trying to figure out how Yoshi could have known where I was that I couldn't come up with a good excuse.

Molasses decided to speak. "Don't be mad at Gatsby. He was just helping me."

Yoshi snorted. Duke laughed out loud and said, "Lady, I know why he went in there. I'm sure that if you asked him to jump into a shark tank to fetch your collar, he'd dive in and we'd all have fish for dinner. I was trying to make a point and the point is —"

"Maury!" I said. "You had Maury the mouse following Molasses! That's how you knew where we were!"

"No." said Yoshi.

"Aw, come on! He's pretty close." squeaked a voice from the darkness. Maury emerged from behind a tree.

"OK, then, who were you following?" I demanded.

Maury looked at Yoshi. Yoshi gave him a nod and Maury answered my question. "I was actually following Smokey."

Yoshi said, "Tell him."

"Yoshi asked me to shadow a cat named Smokey. I picked him up this afternoon after he talked to you guys."

This was weird. Usually this little rat was too intimidated by cats to say two words without stammering. Apparently whatever he had done tonight had filled him with confidence. I'd have to do something about that tomorrow but for now I just listened to his report.

"I tailed my quarry around the neighborhood for a few hours while he did nothing of particular significance."

"C'mon rat!" I said, "Move the story along."

He hesitated for a second, then licked his whiskers and continued, "My subject then met three pit bulldogs and engaged in conversation. I couldn't get close enough to hear what they were saying."

That surprised me. "Whoa! Smokey and those dogs met and had a talk?"

"Yeah, for about five minutes. They all seemed kind of mad. When the conversation broke up, I switched my surveillance to the pit bulls and followed them to this house. They entered the house and stayed inside. I was watching the house when I saw you and Molasses enter. At that point I ran back to report to Yoshi. Then he went out and found Duke."

Yoshi shot me a withering look. "Imagine that," he said. "He saw something potentially dangerous and reported to me."

Molasses turned to me and asked, "Who's Smokey?"

I turned to her and said, "He's a cat who told us that he got attacked by our three dog friends right after you and I first encountered them. He said that they beat him up as a message to me to keep away from you."

"Me? What the heck? I never saw them before that night!"

Yoshi said, "Do you know a cat named Smokey?"

"No."

He asked me to describe Smokey to her.

"Well," I said, "He's a little guy about nine pounds. His color is dark grey which is where I suppose he got his name. His biggest characteristic is his attitude. He's a complete jerk. Mean, nasty and he won't use any clean words if he can think of five or six dirty words that will do just as well. If you don't know him you're not missing a thing. He's just a sour little –"

"You talking about me?" Smokey emerged from around the corner of the house. Preston the German Shepherd was right beside him.

"Thanks for bringing him." Duke told Preston. "Did you have any trouble finding him?"

"Naw, he was in the vicinity just like Yoshi said he would be."

Duke turned to Yoshi. "Okay he's here. Now what?"

"Yeah, what do you want now?" Smokey demanded with all of his usual charm.

"Actually if you don't mind, could you move a little closer to Gatsby? I don't want to have to raise my voice."

Smokey seemed hesitant but Preston growled, "Move it!" and he complied. He walked up until he was a couple feet away from me. This put him close to the house and right in front of the rain barrel. I figured that real reason Yoshi asked him to get closer to me was so that Molasses could get a closer look at him and when

93

I glanced at her I noticed that she did seem to be staring at Smokey very intently.

Smokey didn't even look in her direction. Instead he addressed Duke. "OK, you sent that idiot dog to drag me here. What do you want? I don't know anything about those dogs besides what I already told you!"

Duke growled, "You better watch your mouth! Those pit bulls are now locked up in an animal control facility. I had you brought here because my, um, friend Yoshi is investigating an unrelated matter and thinks that you might know something about it."

All eyes turned to Yoshi. He looked at all of us in turn, from Molasses and me, to Smokey and Preston, to Maury then to Duke and Rowdy. "As most of you know, Gatsby and I were engaged by Miss Molasses to find her brother Butterscotch. So far our efforts have been unsuccessful. I was hoping that Smokey might be able to help us."

Smokey turned up his scowl as far as it could go. "I don't think so!"

Yoshi smiled. "That's ok. I didn't think that this would go the easy way." Then he suddenly shouted, "Now Preston!"

Preston sprung into action. Or at least his butt did as he whacked the rain barrel with his rear end and the barrel fell over. A torrent of water spilled out and drenched Smokey.

Usually any cat in those circumstances would screech and run for the hills. Not Smokey. He just sat there soaked looking at mad as a wet ca-, well he just looked really mad. Then there was something else weird about him. The water had washed out his fur so that he didn't seem charcoal grey anymore. Blackness seemed to be dripping off of him.

"Hey Smokey!" I said "I think your mascara is running."

Molasses said "Butterscotch?"

I could see it now. After having been drenched with the water, Smokey wasn't white, but enough of whatever he had used to disguise himself had come off so that he was now a really light dirty grey but you could tell that he should be white.

Yoshi spoke up. "I'm sorry, but I really couldn't think of a better way to make the truth known."

Smokey or rather Butterscotch just glared at him.

Duke sighed. "OK Yoshi, would you like to tell us how you knew that Smokey was the missing cat?"

Yoshi blinked a couple of times. "Seriously? You guys really didn't know? Gatsby, what was that case you turned down from the Bascom house?"

I replied, "Somebody had knocked over the Bascoms' barbecue grill and their dog Lightning was being blamed for –" I stopped as I realized what he was getting at.

Yoshi continued. "That's right. A white cat disappears, a neighborhood grill is knocked over, leaving a mess of ashes and then a grey cat suddenly shows up. And no one but me drew any kind of conclusion from that?" He slowly shook his head silently bemoaning the fact that he was so much smarter than everyone else.

"Yeah, yeah" Duke snarled. "Go on."

"Well that was the most obvious part. I can guess at everything else and Butterscotch can confirm or deny what he wishes."

Butterscotch just sat there glaring.

Yoshi continued. "My first guess is that Butterscotch ran away from home of his own accord, but he was still keeping tabs on Molasses. When he found out that she was coming to me for help, he must've hired the pit bulls to scare me off. When that didn't work he had them rough him up a little so that he could warn me off in person or get a closer look at me."

Butterscotch snorted.

"Do you have a correction?" Yoshi asked.

"Naw," Butterscotch snarled, "You're telling the story, jerk."

"Oh, that's excellent!" Yoshi said. "That's the attitude that made me suspect that there was something not genuine about you. You were overacting the rough, gruff street cat routine. I've known many stray cats and none were as rude, abrasive or foul-mouthed as you were acting."

He got no reaction from Smokey, so he continued. "Anyway I need to get home so let me just say that there's only one thing that isn't clear. I know you ran away from home and created a secret identity. I know that you hired those pit bulls in an effort to protect your secret identity, probably paying them with the meat that was missing from the Rogers' freezer. I don't know how you met those dogs in the first place, but who cares? What I don't know is your motive. Why did you runaway? Was it the pressure of competing in the cat shows? Was it the primordial thrill of being on your own and surviving on your natural instincts? Well, have you got anything to say for yourself?"

Smokey/Butterscotch stood up and turned to face Molasses. He shook himself a couple of times then stood as tall as he could in an effort to restore some of his dignity. In the full blue glow of the moon he just looked like a dirty, washed out fleabag to me.

He looked at Molasses as if there were no one else there and said, "I did it for love. I did it for you, Mo. I figured that if I wasn't around to compete in the cat show, you could finally win!"

She just looked at him blankly for a few seconds while she digested his explanation. Then she asked, "Then why would you send those pit bulls after me and Gatsby?"

"They weren't going to hurt you; they were just supposed to scare you off. I didn't want to be found until you had won first prize."

I jumped in "So why did you get that beating? There had to be a less painful way to warn us off or get a better look at us."

He gave me a scornful look. "The beating was for real. I told Nails that her performance with you that night was horrible and she beat me up a little."

"You filed a false report with us!" Rowdy squealed. Nobody paid him any attention.

Molasses was ready to speak and she didn't look happy. "So let me make sure that I have this straight. You ran away and scared me and our people half to death because you love me?"

"Yes! And I always have! I know you think of me as just your friend, but-"

She didn't let him finish. "And you actually thought that I'd be happy? You idiot! I don't need you throwing any cat shows for me! I can beat you on my own!"

He answered, "Well, you haven't yet." He probably should've just not said anything.

"Shut Up!" Molasses said, "You're coming home with me right now!"

All of the gruffness and obnoxiousness had jumped right out of Butterscotch. He seemed embarrassed as he began to walk away. Molasses was right on his heels. She turned her head to give me a wink and said, "I'll see you around."

Smokey/Butterscotch also turned his head to give me a glare.

"What are you looking at?" Mo asked him. "Keep walking! You just wait we get home!"

We could hear her berating him long after they had disappeared into the woods.

Things had quieted down. While we were in back chatting, the cops had just about finished up and most of the cars had driven off, taking the flashing lights with them. The only light source now was the big blue moon floating above our heads.

Maury the mouse spoke up. "Well, I've got to go. I can't wait to tell the wife how I saved Gatsby's life!"

That surprised me "You saved my what?"

"Well, you know, if I hadn't told Yoshi where you were, you would have been, uh, well those pit bulls would have chewed you up!"

You mean like this?" I said as I pounced at him. I purposely landed at least a foot away from him but he didn't notice and took off running in fright. I yelled to his back that he'd better not go around telling anybody that he saved my life.

Yoshi said, "It may hurt your pride but he's right, you know."

"Yeah," I replied, "Now you're going to start. I know you're going to lay into me for not reporting back about this house."

He smiled. "Not at all. The enemies that you made tonight should be enough to teach you a lesson."

"What are you talking about?"

"Well, Butterscotch is pretty mad. Much angrier at you than he is at me. And he's extremely clever. I'd advise staying away from him, although that won't be possible if you're going to keep seeing Molasses.

I scoffed, "I can handle anybody named Butterscotch."

"Sure but what about Nails and her two lackeys. They're sure to hold a huge grudge against you."

I laughed. "What about them? They're in jail!"

Yoshi's smile turned into a smirk. "Until they escape."

Duke, who had been watching our discussion with amusement, took offence at that remark. "Animals do not escape from Animal Control!"

Yoshi wasn't impressed. "Except for all of the ones who have. What about Cinnamon, that cat we caught poisoning the Richardson's dogs? He broke out of the County Animal Shelter. And you'll remember Hector and Jesse, those stray dogs who were terrorizing the mailman. Were they even locked up for a whole day before they'd escaped? That Animal Control building might as well install revolving doors!"

Duke and Preston were both looking very irritated with Yoshi's disrespect of the Animal Control prison.

Yoshi turned back to me. "Anyway, maybe having to constantly watch your back for these new enemies will teach you a lesson. It's inexcusable that on Halloween night I had to come outside to save your neck!"

"You can stop." I interrupted. I could hear some people hanging around the front of the house. "I really do appreciate you braving the horrible outdoors just to help me out. I just hope those Goth kids I just saw up front don't come back here and see you. They'd probably love to get their hands on a black cat tonight. Who knows what kind of weird Halloween rituals they would use you for and -" I stopped speaking as I had turned to face Yoshi and he was no longer where he had been sitting.

Duke looked at me. "He got up and started running as soon as you said the word Goth."

I grinned back at him "He was probably at home under the bed by the time I said 'rituals'".

Preston was usually too authoritarian to laugh at my nonsense, especially when Duke was around but this was too much. We both cracked up. Duke said, "You'd think that he would've realized that the people up front are just the last cops finishing up."

As if on cue we heard a voice calling from up front. "Duke! C'mon boy! Where are you?" It was Deputy Bishop, Duke's owner.

Duke turned to Preston. "We gotta go." Then he looked at me. "Hey kid, you've had a rough night. Do you need a lift home?"

I shook my head. "Nope. I can walk. I'll see you guys later." I watched as Duke and Preston trotted up to the front of the house. After a couple of seconds, a car door slammed and the last SUV drove off leaving the house.

Everything was quiet. The best route home was to cut through the woods. I wasn't in a hurry as Yoshi was sure to be in a foul mood. I just walked through the trees at a slow, leisurely pace as the blue moon shone down on me and I thought about how soon would be too soon to go see Molasses again.

THE END

Robert J. Smith

PETECTIVES: CHRISTMAS PARTY

CHAPTER 1

It was late December and the sounds of jingle bells filled the air. The bells weren't coming from any horse drawn sleighs but from the stupid bell on the collar that the little girl that I lived with had put on me last night. The collar was a red and green striped nylon strap with a black plastic clasp and a brass bell on the front directly under my chin. I didn't mind the people putting a collar around my neck, but what was the point of the bell?

I found the ringing from the bell to be highly annoying as I walked along the suburban sidewalks on my way to an appointment. It was an extremely cold night that made me grateful that I'd been born with a thick, orange striped coat. A severe ice storm had hit earlier that day and everything looked like it was coated with thick, clear glass. It was as if the houses and trees were glazed donuts and it made everything outside look beautiful, especially the houses that had Christmas lights. The ice seemed to heighten the effect of the colorful lights, making them even brighter and cheerier against the dark winter night. Despite all of the beauty, the ice had caused some damage and every so often I had to walk around a fallen tree branch or even a downed tree. The power had gone out at my house for a couple of hours, but since my people had left town to visit relatives for the Christmas holiday, nobody had really been inconvenienced.

Actually the atmosphere inside my house had gotten pretty icy as well. Our people had gone to visit relatives and wouldn't be back until after Christmas. The house was just occupied by me and my housemate Yoshi, which gave me the idea that we should throw a big Christmas party for all of the neighborhood animals.

"Absolutely not." Yoshi had said when I'd presented the idea to him a couple of hours ago. "I won't have every filthy dog and cat in the area wreaking havoc on my house."

This seemed a little strident to me since I lived there too, but he was older which made him the alpha cat and therefore what he says goes. Or so he thought. "Oh, come on," I replied, "Every pet left behind by their family wants to throw a huge party. Let's live the dream."

"Let's not"

"C'mon, where's your Christmas spirit?"

At that point he rolled his eyes at me and said, "What do you know about Christmas spirit? What do you know about Christmas?"

"What don't I know? I've watched about fifty gazillion Christmas specials with the kids. I know everything about Christmas."

"I doubt that," he answered. "Christmas means a bit more than what you're likely to absorb from the pabulum fed to you from children's television. In any event we will not be having a party in this house. "

I kept trying and he kept denying and the end result was that when I left the house for my appointment, he and I were barely on speaking terms. Hopefully my meeting would lead to an interesting case which would ease some of the tension between the two of us.

My meeting was on the corner of Fillmore and Pershing, in front of a house with a lit-up seven foot tall inflated snowman. Classy. I was about a block away and I could see a cat standing in the snow about five feet in front of the decoration.

As I got closer, I got a better look at her. She was a bit older than me, but the years were treating her very well. She was a medium sized brown cat with black patches on her back and belly. Although her fur was heavier than mine, she looked like she was freezing.

"Penelope?" I called as I trotted across the lawn towards her. The footing was much better on the lawn than it had been on the iced over sidewalks.

She nodded. "Please call me Penny. You must be the cat who works for Yoshi."

"I work with Yoshi," I corrected her, "It's not like he pays me."

She raised her eye whiskers. "I didn't mean to offend you."

I smiled at her to show her that we were friends. "You didn't. Now what did you want to see me about?"

She hesitated for a second and then said, "I hate to say it, but I was kind of hoping that Yoshi would show up with you."

I laughed. "Lady, the only appointments Yoshi shows up for are mealtimes and naptimes. And he wouldn't show up for those if they were outside of our house."

"That doesn't sound like the Yoshi I used to know." She said doubtfully, as if she thought that I was lying. I might have taken offense at that, if I hadn't been so intrigued by the last four words of her sentence.

"You used to know Yoshi?" I asked. "When?"

"Oh, I used to live in this neighborhood." She said. "My girl went to college about five years ago and I went with her. She hasn't been able to find a job since she graduated so we moved back in with her parents a couple of weeks ago."

"Well, welcome back. So can I help you with something? Or did you just want to talk about old times with Yoshi?"

"No, I've got a problem. I think that someone is trying to kill my friend. About a week ago –". She stopped talking and gave me an odd look. I realized that I had a big grin on my face.

"Sorry," I said, "I'm not happy that someone's trying to kill your friend. It's just that my life's been kind of boring for the last couple of months. The prospect of stopping someone from doing away with someone else makes me a little enthusiastic."

She looked doubtful. "Doesn't that mean that you are in fact happy that someone's trying to kill my friend?"

I started to reply but before the words came out of my mouth she said, "Never mind. I suppose that it's good that you're enthusiastic about your work. Can I continue?"

I saw no point in saying anything so I nodded.

She continued. "About a week ago, Thor, the dog that I live with got sick. Violently ill. He would've died if our people hadn't gotten him to the vet in time."

"Sounds bad."

"It was, they had to pump his stomach."

"Is he okay?" I asked.

"He is now. He spent a couple of days at the animal hospital but he seems alright now."

"How did the poison get into him?"

"There was a piece of bologna on the ground in the backyard. He said that it smelled funny but he ate it anyway. Apparently it had been soaked in some kind of liquid fertilizer."

She was interrupted when a harsh wind blew at us. When things had quieted down, I asked, "Why would he eat the bologna if it smelled funny?"

She shrugged. "It was a piece of bologna. He's on a special diet so he doesn't get to eat anything other than dry dog food. He jumps at any treat that he sees." Then she cocked her head and said, "Listen."

The wind had died down and the night was very still. All I could hear was a couple of dogs a couple of blocks away, loudly barking. One dog was much louder than the other. They seemed to be debating the merits of drinking water from a hose versus gulping it out of the toilet.

"Is he one of the dogs engaged in the philosophy discussion?" I asked.

"Yep. Loud, isn't he?"

"A little. You must get a lot of noise complaints – from Russia."

She smiled. "He can be loud and opinionated. Even obnoxious. But he's the most loyal friend you could ever have." The smile went away. "Somebody tried to hurt him. I want to know who."

"I think we can help you."

"Great!" she perked up again, "Come with me and I'll introduce you to Thor."

"Whoa, I can't tonight. I have a previous engagement. How about I drop by your house tomorrow morning around ten?"

"That would be great! Maybe Yoshi could come and – "

"I doubt that," I interrupted. "I don't know what he was like five years ago but like I said before,   Yoshi is strictly an indoor cat. He wouldn't leave our house unless it was on fire and even then it would be under protest."

"He sounds so different. Maybe I'll come around sometime and see him."

"Sure, you do that. I'll see you tomorrow morning."

"That's fine." She smiled again. "I'll see you tomorrow." She winked at me and strolled off in the direction of the dog barking.

I watched her for a minute and then took off in the opposite direction

CHAPTER 2

I was in a pretty good mood as I strolled off to my next appointment. We now had a client with an interesting case and the interview hadn't made me late for my date.

My good mood was somewhat broken when I got about five houses away from my destination and I didn't smell the girl I was going to meet. If she was where she was supposed to be, I would've caught her scent by now, even in this frosty air. Where was she? I didn't have to wonder for long. I could hear a big commotion from behind the houses I was walking past. Barking and hissing and spitting that was even loud enough to drown out the bell around my neck. The one doing all of the hissing was my date, the one and only Molasses. I took off and ran up the driveway that I happened to be in front of at full speed, or as full as I could get with all of the ice that covered all of the driveways and lawns. I headed back between two houses and when I got to the backyard I jumped very carefully onto an ice coated chain link fence and ran a few feet down it until I could get a good view of what was happening.

The full moon reflecting off of all the ice illuminated a grim scene. A chase was approaching me. It was about four backyards away and coming fast but I could clearly see two cats being chased by a vicious dog. I recognized two out of the three participants. The cat running in the lead was my girlfriend. She was a medium sized cat, white with black patches and cute as a button even while running for her life. Her name was Molasses and at this particular moment her name seemed ironic as she was moving faster than I'd ever seen a cat move. Running right next to her was a kitten that I didn't recognize. He had no collar and was orange, but not as orange and stripey as me. His tiny legs were pumping hard to keep up with Molasses.

The dog chasing them was someone I knew well. He was a bulldog named Percy who was usually chained to the railing on his back porch. As fast as he was running, I could still see the chain dangling from his neck trailing on the ground behind his grey muscled body. He had been threatening to break free for years and apparently it had finally happened. The most likely explanation for what was happening was that Percy had been going after the kitten, Molasses had come along and tried to defend the little guy and now Percy was trying to turn them both into chew toys.

I was pretty sure that the only thing that was going to distract Percy from his prey was more desirable prey. I certainly fit that description, having spent years mocking him from beyond the range of his chain. I knew that he would love to sink his teeth into me. There was only one thing to do.

I was still atop the chain link fence and I stood as best I could while making sure that I didn't slip on the icy surface. The procession was only a backyard away from me and approaching fast.

"Hey Percival!" I shouted. "What's up, dog?"

The chase instantly stopped. At least Percy did. Molasses and her friend kept running. The both of them kept going, vaulted the fence that I was standing on and hit the ground running on the other side. Percy had lost interest in them and was glaring at me.

"Gatsby! Oh, I'm going to enjoy this." He said in a tone that clearly implied that I wasn't going to be enjoying anything ever again.

"Merry Christmas!" I said in as cheery a voice I could manage.

"I guess that I was an extra good boy this year!" He growled, "Getting a hold of you has been on my Christmas list for years."

Molasses and company were long gone at this point. I was free to put my plan in action. The plan that I had hastily conceived in three seconds that probably wouldn't work. It occurred to me that it might be a better idea to try talking to him

"So, Percy," I began. That was actually all that I managed to get out as he picked that moment to attack.

He jumped five feet in the air right at me. There's no way he should've been able to jump that high but I guess that shows how much he hated me. As soon as I saw him tense up to jump at me, I leapt off of the fence, hitting the ice covered ground running. I headed back the way I had come, even stepping in the same footprints I had made when I had been running towards the fence. Percy was hot on my heels which was weird. There was no way a bulldog should have been as fast as me but he was right on my tail and would probably catch me in a second or two. The best guess was that his legs were being powered by all the years of frustration that my taunts from just beyond the range of his chain had caused.

In an instant we had covered the thirty feet from the fence that I'd been sitting on to the house's driveway. As soon as I got to the edge of the driveway, I leapt straight up into the air and executed a perfectly timed back flip. Percy ran right beneath me. When he realized that I was no longer in front of him, he tried to spin around to get back after me. Sadly for him spinning around on a driveway coated with about a half inch of ice wasn't easy. As soon as he tried to turn, he lost his footing and began to slip. I watched his face as it went from an expression of horrible anger to absolute horror.

I had complained earlier that it was a steep climb to get to the backyard of that house but now it was a pleasure to see Percy slipping and sliding down that slickened driveway. After he'd gone about three feet, he collapsed, fell on his belly and started spinning around with his paws outstretched. He went down the driveway until I couldn't see him and I assume that from there he slid out into the street and wouldn't stop until he hit the curb on the opposite side. But he heard me exclaim as he slid out of sight, "Merry Christmas, Fool! And to all a good night!"

I realize that that may have been a bit much, but what the hey, it's Christmas.

CHAPTER 3

I caught up with Molasses about three blocks away. She and her kitten friend were walking across the lawns of another residential street.

"Hey, what was that all about?" I asked as I approached them.

Molasses glanced down at her companion and then answered, "All I know is that Percy got loose and was chasing this little guy."

At close quarters the little guy looked a little different. He was orange like me but he had a white shock of fur on his chest and matched the white on all four of his paws. I would have guessed him to be about four months old. He was certainly skinny, even for a kitten. I wondered when was the last time he'd eaten. "Hey little guy. What's your name?"

"Nothing." He said quietly as he stared at the ground.

"Nothing?" I asked Molasses.

"He doesn't seem to have a name." She said.

"Not much of a talker, is he?"

"That's ok," she said as she gave him a reassuring smile. "I like my men strong and silent."

That should have gotten a smile out him. Or an embarrassed grimace. Or at the very least, a shrug. He had no reaction whatsoever; he just kept looking at the ground.

Molasses continued, "Percy must have finally broken loose from his chain and was chasing this cute little guy. I tried to help and you saw the result of that."

"Cute?" I repeated. I looked at the kitten. "Hey dude, are you trying to steal my girlfriend?"

I was just messing with him to see if I could get a reaction. He just kept studying the frosted grass between his paws.

Molasses broke the silence. "Don't be silly," she said, "We need to get him off of the streets. He's been roaming around by himself for the last few days."

"In this weather?" I said incredulously, "He must be a tough little nut."

That got a reaction out of the kitten. The corners of his mouth went up in what I took to be a quick flash of a grin. If I had blinked I would have missed it but he definitely smiled.

Just then we were given a harsh reminder of exactly where we were and what time of the year it was. A savage wind that must have originated in the Arctic and travelled down through Alaska and Canada blasted right through us.

"Whoa," I exclaimed after the wind had died down, "This is not weather for cats to be out and about in. Where can we drop this kid off so we can go back to my house?"

Molasses just looked at me.

"You want to take him with us?"

She smiled her special smile at me. This had the effect of making me feel much warmer. "Well," she said, "I was hoping that maybe he could stay with you for a couple of days."

I was aghast. "What! Are you kidding?"

"Oh, why not? Your people are out of town until after Christmas. It's just you and Yoshi in that big house."

"Oh!" I exclaimed. "What's Yoshi going to say if I bring home some strange kitten that I hardly know? He'll freak out!"

"I'd take him to my house but my people are there and you know that Butterscotch would be mean to him!"

Butterscotch was the sour little cat that lived with Molasses. He didn't like most other creatures in general and me in specific. I imagined that he would not like this kitten at all. I had begun to change my mind about bringing him to my house. With the way that Yoshi and I had been fighting, there was no telling how he would react if I brought home a stray kitten. There was the potential for some hilarity.

"OK." I said, "He's coming home with me."

CHAPTER 4

My house was quiet when Molasses, the kitten and I arrived. We'd only gotten a couple of steps inside when I heard the sound of Yoshi's paws bounding down the stairs. He met us in the living room and his sleek, jet black body was as tense as a bowstring. He had instantly known that there was a strange cat in the house with Molasses and me and he was doing his best to control himself but I could see that his tail was all puffy.

"Who have you brought into my house?" He demanded.

"Now take it easy," I said, "You know Molasses."

"I'm not talking about Molasses! Who is he?"

Molasses smiled her nicest smile. "Hello Yoshi."

While the smile didn't have quite the same effect on Yoshi as it did on me, he did calm down a little. "Hello Molasses. I apologize for my manners. Maybe you will be so good as to tell me who this is."

The kitten spoke up. "I don't have a name."

We all stared at him for a moment but he didn't say anything else. I figured that I'd better speak up. "I've decided to call him Chuck." I said.

Yoshi rolled his eyes. "Fine. He's Chuck. Why is he in my house?" Now he seemed more exasperated than angry. It was a perfect time for me for me to explain the situation.

"Let me explain," I said, "I came across Percy chasing Molasses and this little guy. I distracted Percy so that they could escape. Apparently Chuck has lost his family and has been on the streets for a couple of days. That's pretty much all that I know about him."

Yoshi looked him over for a second and then said "I'd say that he's three and a half months old, he weighs a two pounds and he's been on the streets for three days, judging from the state of his coat. Also he ate out of our garbage yesterday. I can smell that dreadful Chicken Marsala that our woman made on his breath."

"Oh stop showing off." The situation seemed a bit less tense so I looked at Molasses and Chuck and nodded at the fireplace. "C'mon guys."

They followed me to the fireplace. It wasn't real but one of those fancy gas contraptions. All you had to do was flip a switch and you got a nice natural gas fire on some fake logs behind a glass pane. It generated a good amount of heat, just the thing for three cats that had been outside in horrible winter weather.

Molasses sat down on the carpet facing the fire. I plopped down next to her and Chuck carefully sat next to me. During his walk across the room his eyes never left our Christmas tree. I couldn't blame him, the tree was very impressive, towering six feet above us and adorned with all kinds of glass and plastic ornaments. When I was Chuck's age I liked climbing the Christmas tree and even knocked it over once or twice but now I was used to it. I was trying to remember the first time I'd seen a Christmas tree when I noticed Yoshi staring at me.

"Comfortable?" He asked in a tone that would have seemed sincere to Molasses and Chuck but that I knew was sarcastic. He had sat down facing us with the fire behind him. Not giving me a chance to answer, he continued. "Now who is going to tell me about this kitten? He's obviously too young to speak for himself."

Chuck spoke up. "I can speak just fine." A victory for reverse psychology.

Yoshi followed up. "Well then speak. Do you have a name? Where are you from?"

For a second Chuck looked as if he might go back into shy mode. He didn't. "I don't have a name. I was at a pet shelter with my mom and sisters. I didn't like them so I left."

Yoshi raised hid eye whiskers. "You left the shelter and ran away into the bitter cold because you didn't like your siblings? That's hard to believe."

Chuck just stared at him.

Yoshi continued. "Did they hurt you?"

"No."

"Did the humans there hurt you?"

"No."

"How about the food? How was it?"

Chuck's face made a little grimace. "Pretty bad."

"Was there enough to go around?"

"Not really."

Yoshi was quiet for a moment. "Hmm. I assume that Gatsby brought you here to warm yourself. However Percy is still probably out there roaming around loose and if he isn't properly dealt with, he can be a problem. How would you like to stay here with us for a couple of days?"

Chuck looked at me and then Molasses before answering. "Sure. Thanks."

Molasses stared at me with a shocked expression on her face and I suppose that I was staring back at her with the same look on my face. We had been sure that Yoshi was going to put up a huge fight and would probably throw Chuck out and me with him. Now here he was inviting Chuck to stay. I've heard people talk about Christmas miracles but that was the first one that I'd ever witnessed.

CHAPTER 5

The next morning was Christmas Eve but I didn't get the day off. A little before ten o'clock Chuck and I went out to work. It was noticeably warmer than the night before and the sun was out and shining on all of the ice caked houses and trees. Most of the sidewalks were icy although some industrious people had shoveled or put down rock salt. Chuck and I kept to travelling over lawns.

Last night after Molasses had left and Chuck had fallen asleep I told Yoshi all about that night's events. I covered everything in detail from meeting Penelope to my brief encounter with Percy to my first meeting with Chuck. Yoshi seemed bored with what I had to say but I knew that he was listening to every word. When I was done he didn't have any questions, which was a sign that I had done a good job. I, on the other hand had a couple of questions about Penelope and the nature of her and Yoshi's relationship. He refused to answer any questions about her saying that while he did know her in the past, that couldn't have anything to do with the matter at hand. When I had first mentioned her name and that she knew him, his attitude toward her seemed pretty nonchalant. That fit in with his general personality, she could have either been the love of his life or somebody he hardly knew and he would've acted the same.

As I was leaving that morning I asked Chuck if he wanted to come along and he said yes. He had slept for about eleven hours and looked much better than he had the night before. For a cat there is nothing better for health than a good night's sleep. Or a good day's sleep. Or any sleep at all. Anyway, after Chuck woke up, I shared my breakfast with him and we were ready to go. Yoshi couldn't understand cats voluntarily going outdoors into freezing temperatures but he told us goodbye before heading off for his regularly scheduled ten o'clock nap.

After we'd walked about three blocks I noticed that Chuck was very interested in the various holiday decorations on some of the houses that we passed. He didn't ask about them but I could tell that he was curious. A couple of blocks later he did have a question. "What are we going to do?"

"Well," I said, "Last night a cat told me that the dog she lives with got poisoned. She'd like us to find out who did the poisoning and stop them from doing it again. We're going to talk to the dog and some of the animals in his neighborhood to see if we can figure out what happened."

"Why do you care? It's none of your business, is it?"

"It's better than sitting around the house licking myself all day."

I'm not sure that he agreed with my last statement but he didn't say anything. At this point we were pretty close to our destination. We could hear a couple of dogs nearby in a heated argument. Their frenzied barking was loud enough to be heard from miles around. I couldn't tell what the argument was about but you could tell that strong emotions were involved. I glanced at Chuck. "Well, speaking of me not minding my own business, let's go see what up with these dogs."

The sound of the dog fight was coming from behind a red brick split level house. 59 Fillmore Drive. Chuck shot a look at me. "Isn't this the house where we were going to meet your friend?"

"Yep," I replied, "One of those dogs must be our buddy, Thor. Let's get back there quietly and maybe we can hear what they're fighting about."

We trotted up the driveway and into the backyard. The house had a huge patio and we stopped beside a lawn chair. The dogs were too immersed in their argument to notice our arrival. One dog was in the same backyard as Chuck and me while the other dog was in the backyard of the house directly behind, the two dogs separated by a chain link fence. The dog in the yard with us matched Penelope's description of Thor, a big black Lab with a loud booming bark. He was arguing with a Doberman Pincher, which seemed like a bad idea to me but Thor didn't seem intimidated in the least.

"You keep away from my girl!" the Doberman was barking. This dog was almost frothing at the mouth with anger.

"I've got nothing to do with your girl!" The Lab snarled back. "Or maybe I do. What are you going to do about it?"

That set the Doberman off on a tirade full of language that I don't think that I should repeat here. The Lab just sat back and smiled.

Penelope the cat walked up to Chuck and me. "Enjoying the show?" she asked in a low whisper.

"Yeah," I responded. "What's going on?"

Penelope eyed Chuck. "Who's this little guy?"

"He's my assistant. The workload's been getting too heavy for me so I got an intern."

She didn't seem impressed. "How nice for you. We need to talk. Something happened."

I grinned at her. "I figured that out from the Doberman wanting to rip your friend to shreds. What happened?"

She didn't grin back. "Somebody left Missy a Christmas present. There was a big rawhide bone left in her backyard this morning."

"Who's Missy?" I asked.

"She's a dog who lives over there". Penelope nodded over towards a house and yard positioned diagonal to the yard we were in. It was the house next door to the Doberman's. "All of the male dogs around here find her fascinating." Her tone of voice clearly indicated that she didn't see what was so special about Missy.

I began to see what was going on. "So the Doberman thinks that she's his and his alone and he's thinking that your buddy Thor is leaving her presents so that he can steal her away."

"You got it."

"Does the Doberman actually have a reason why he thinks that Thor left the bone? While I'm asking, does the Doberman have a name?"

"His name is Zabisco."

That took me aback. "Zabisco? Are you serious?"

"That's his name. About the bone-"

I couldn't get off of the subject of his name. "Zabisco? That's insane! Why would people name him that? What does that even mean?"

Penelope looked like she might be getting a little annoyed with me. "I really don't know."

"I guess it explains his obvious anger management issues, but–"

Chuck jumped in with a question to get the conversation back on track. "Um, why does Zabisco think that your friend gave her the bone?"

She gave him a huge smile. "Thank you for getting us focused. It was actually Thor's bone. Our people gave it to him yesterday. Missy says that his scent is all over it."

I was wondering what the big deal was. "So he regifted it to Zabisco's girlfriend."

"No, he didn't. It was left early this morning and I know that Thor didn't leave the house since he came in last night. Someone

140

else left it at Missy's, probably to anger Zabisco. It's another mystery."

Great, another mystery was just what we needed. Usually I hate when complications like this occur. I would rather show up at the scene of whatever incident I'm investigating, ask some questions, examine the location and figure out what happened (well, usually I go home and tell Yoshi everything and he figures out what happened). I like things to be nice and simple. Yoshi on the other hand, loves when things like this happens. He says that something like this is a sign that somebody is getting way too cute and is likely to give themselves away.

There was a positive aspect in that I had somebody to focus on. If Thor had been trying to move in on Zabisco's girlfriend, then Zabisco would definitely be motivated to leave him poisoned bologna.

Looking at Penelope I said, "I'm going to need to chat with Thor, Zabisco, this canine temptress and any other animals in the neighborhood that have anything to do with Thor. I need to see where Thor found this bologna and where he kept this bone and where Zabisco's girlfriend found it. Is all of that doable?"

"Sure." She replied. "I'll introduce you to Thor in just a minute. First, can I ask you a question?"

"Shoot."

"Did Yoshi say anything about me when you told him that you met me last night?"

It took a lot of self-control not to laugh but I managed. I don't know what had happened between her and Yoshi all those years ago but she sure had it bad.

"Yeah," I lied, "He said that you and he should get together and talk about old times."

Another cat came up to us from around the corner of the house. "Who's Yoshi?" He asked. He was a medium sized chestnut brown cat with really big black eyes.

"Hi Morris." Penny greeted him. She didn't seem glad to see him. "Yoshi is an old friend of mine."

The cat, who apparently was named Morris looked me over for a second. "And who would this be?" He sounded like this was his world and why was I in it? While I realize that this is a common attitude among cats (Heck, I deal with it everyday from Yoshi), I didn't appreciate it and I had already decided that I didn't like this cat.

I smiled at him anyway. "My name's Gatsby. This is my associate, Chuck. We're new friends of hers."

Penny chimed in. "They investigate things. I asked them to look into what happened to Thor."

His eyes widened. "You mean you're still telling people that he got poisoned? Really? He gets a little food poisoning and first you call that German Shepard to pester us and now this?"

She replied, "Yes. Really."

"What German Shepard?" I asked although I had a bad feeling that I knew the answer.

Penny sighed. "I asked the Dog Patrol to look into this before I thought of you and Yoshi."

I sighed. Yoshi wasn't going to like this. The Dog Patrol was a group of four dogs led by a gruff ex-police dog named Duke. They thought of themselves as the police force for the animal contingent of our neighborhood and if they had been sniffing around this case before me, who knows how they might have messed things up. "What did they do?"

"Nothing, really. Duke came around and talked to me and Thor and Morris about what happened.   Then he told me that he'd be back. That was three days ago."

"Hmm."

She suddenly looked concerned. "Hmm? What does 'hmm' mean?"

"It's an interjection." I answered, "It usually indicates thoughtful absorption, doubt or puzzlement."

That stopped the conversation dead. Penelope and Morris both stared at me for a few seconds the Penelope said, "You've definitely been hanging around Yoshi."

I decided to skip any comments about my weird tendency to define interjections and ask Morris a few questions. "OK Morris, let's just humor the lady about this whole someone's trying to kill Thor thing. If someone was trying to murder him, who would it be?"

Morris's perpetual smirk turned into a full laugh. "He's the most obnoxious beast I've ever met in my life! Everybody hates him! How's that?"

"Could you be a little more specific?"

"How about Zabisco over there?" He said, referring to the Doberman that was currently yelling at Thor. "He would love to live in a world without Thor."

I looked at Penelope. "Just because he thinks that Thor left her a bone?"

"Ha! It's a little more than that!" Morris was apparently full of gossip. "Zabisco and Missy have been a couple since they were puppies. Everybody in the neighborhood knew that. Then a couple of weeks ago, Zabisco's supposed best friend Thor starts talking all romantic to her. Thor's been telling everybody he knows that he and Missy are now a couple. Z's going crazy from jealousy and he's been yelling at Thor for the past two weeks and Thor just laughs at him.

"Sorry, I'm getting a little confused." I told him. "You just said that you don't think that anyone's trying to kill Thor, she told me that he's got no enemies and now you're saying that this Zabisco has a great reason to feed Thor a little poison."

"Look at Zabisco." Morris said.

I gazed at the dogs yapping at each other at the back of the yard. Zabisco was practically frothing at the mouth, barking a particularly nasty insult about Thor's mother. As he barked his body moved in violent motion as he ran around and jumped at the fence. "He looks like he wants to tear out Thor's heart and show it to him."

"Exactly." Morris said with a smirk that would rate an eleven on a smug meter that went up to ten.

I looked at Penelope. "Morris is saying that Zabisco isn't the type to poison someone. He's likely to be a lot more direct and violent. Does that sound right to you?"

She didn't even take a minute to think before responding. "Yes. I told you that I didn't know of anyone that would poison Thor."

"You told me that Thor didn't have any enemies." I answered. "The animals in this neighborhood seem very contradictory."

Morris grinned. "We're just complex."

Penelope was thinking. "So is it possible that whoever left that rawhide bone with Missy assumed that it would infuriate Zabisco and that he would attack Thor? Or maybe Zabisco left the bone there so he would have a good reason to attack Thor.

"OK," I said. "Leave the theories to Yoshi and me. You're giving me a headache. So who else is in the 'I hate Thor' club?"

"Well there's Missy. She wasn't too happy about Thor telling everybody that he'd stolen her from Zabisco." Morris stopped and let loose with a yawn. It was a long loud yawn, the kind of yawn that a cat who hadn't slept in two years might make. "She had talked to him a few times and then their people all went to the park together and brought her and Thor along. Apparently

Thor thought that was a date and the next thing you know he's telling everybody that they're a couple. She didn't like that at all."

This sounded like a promising motive for dogicide. "How mad was she?"

"Oh she read him the riot act, all right. But it didn't matter. Her relationship with Zabisco hasn't been the same since. Trust issues."

"Ah, so would she be likely to poison the dude that caused those trust issues?" I asked hopefully. Maybe I should target my attention on Missy.

"Ha! No way!" He sneered, crushing my hopes. "Missy's a gentle soul. She wouldn't harm a fly. Literally. I once saw her ignore a fly that was all over her butt –"

"Fine." I was getting annoyed. "You seem to be telling me that everybody hates this dog but nobody would be so impolite as to poison him."

Morris rolled his eyes. "Yes, I suppose that is what I'm saying. But so what?"

"So what?"

"Yeah. If you'll pardon the expression, aren't you barking up the wrong tree?"

"Howso?"

He sighed. "Poisoning isn't exactly something one animal would do to another is it? Isn't that more of a human thing?"

"I suppose so," I agreed. "I also suppose that you would have an idea as to which human would want to poison him?"

"Oh, all of them."

"All of them?" For somebody who didn't think that Thor was poisoned, Morris sure thought that a bunch of people wanted him dead. I was still learning a lot more from him than I had from Penelope. Yoshi often told me that the feline detective's best source of information was the gossipiest cat in the neighborhood.

Morris sighed again. "As you can tell, Thor is a loudmouth. His people leave him outside a lot. Day and night."

I turned to Penelope. "Have there been a lot of complaints?"

"Yes," she replied. "Thor keeps a lot of people from getting to sleep at night."

"And he wakes them up too early in the morning. Also he keeps some of us awake during the day." Morris let loose with a huge yawn as if to punctuate his statement. "Look it's been fun sitting out here telling you all of this for no particular reason but I'm going inside now to warm up and maybe even get some sleep."

He gave Penelope a nod and then got up and trotted back towards the house. After he entered I asked Penelope, "Is there a reason that you didn't tell me any of that?"

"I was going to tell you more today. I thought that I'd get a chance to talk to you before you spoke to anyone else. And some of what he just told you I didn't know. I haven't been back in town very long."

I was skeptical. "Morris didn't tell you all of that? He seems pretty forthcoming. Another couple of minutes and he would've given me his owners credit card number complete with the PIN. Do you two not talk?"

She sighed. "Morris doesn't gossip with me. He has other ideas that he thinks he and I should discuss. I'm not interested."

"Oh. Well I still think that you would've —" I trailed off in mid-sentence as I noticed angry dog eyes glaring at me. Thor had finally noticed that there were intruders in his backyard. He had the makings of a truly great watchdog.

"Hey!" he barked, "Get out of my yard!"

Penelope stepped towards him. "They're with me, Thor."

Thor strode towards us. He was a big dog and he seemed to get bigger with every step that brought him closer. "What are they doing here?" he demanded, eyeing Chuck and me with suspicion.

"They're here to help us." Penelope said. "They can find out who tried to poison you."

Dogs have good hearing. Not as good as a cat but still very good. So even though Penelope had kept her voice fairly low

Zabisco must have heard every word. No sooner than the words had come out of Penelope's mouth than we could hear Zabisco laughing.

"Hey Thor," he yelled, "Are those cats here to protect you? Which one's tougher, the orange one or the kitten?"

Thor grimaced and then glared at Penelope. "I need to talk to you for a minute," he said and then they walked to the other side of the house.

I looked down at Chuck. "That's not going to be a pleasant conversation. Let's go talk to the other dog."

He nodded. He and I approached the fence.

"Hey, tough guys!" Zabisco was still in a joking mood. "What's up?"

I gave him my most charming smile. "Hi. My name is Gatsby and this is my friend Chuck."

The dog's eyes narrowed. "Gatsby? I've heard of you. Don't you work for Yoshi?"

"I work with Yoshi. With. You know him?"

"Yeah. He used to come around here. I haven't seen him in a few years, not since he and Penny shut down Jacko the mole's catnapping scam."

I was shocked. "Yoshi and Penny?"

"They used to be tight. They had some kind of fight and then she left town. I heard that he never leaves his house anymore, he has an errand boy that he sends out to-" he paused. "Hey, if you're ok with Yoshi, you're ok with me. What do you want to talk to me about?"

Since he knew perfectly well what I wanted to talk to him about, I thought I'd ask about something other than Thor. "How about the weather? It feels pretty warm after last night."

He pointed his nose to the sky and took a deep sniff. "Enjoy it while you can," he stated. "There's a storm coming. A big storm."

"Penelope thinks that somebody tried to poison Thor. She asked Yoshi and me to look into it. What do you think?"

Robert J. Smith

He flashed a devious smile that made me glad that I was on the other side of a chain link fence. "If I was going to kill him, I wouldn't mess with poison. I'd go right for his throat"

"Yeah," I agreed, "You do seem like straightforward type. But from what I've heard, you're not the only one around here who has a problem with Thor."

"You got that right. He's annoyed just about everybody in this neighborhood. I could believe that a human would try to take him down. He's a pain in the -. Did you hear that?"

His ears perked up and he turned to the house next door to him. Another dog had run out of that house and into the yard next to Zabisco and diagonal to the yard I was occupying. Zabisco's attention was fully occupied by this dog.

"Is that Missy?" I asked.

"Uh Huh" was all the answer that Z could muster.

I could understand the attraction. She was a big Irish Setter with a thick red coat that looked like it had just been brushed. Her bright eyes swept the area, settling on Zabisco and me for a millisecond before continuing around the yard. She walked over to a tree situated at the corner of her yard furthest from Zabisco.

Zabisco sighed and then turned back to me. "Are you going to talk to her too?"

"I'm going to try."

"Can you do me a favor?" His tone had gone from menacing to needy.

"Will it hurt?"

"No."

"Will it cost me anything?"

"No."

"Will it take a lot a time?"

"No! Can you help me out or not?"

"Sure," I said, "What do you need?"

He grimaced. "Just tell her that I'm sorry."

"No problem. What exactly are you sorry about? Are you just a sorry excuse for a dog or is there something in particular that you're sorry about?"

Chuck lived up to his name and chuckled. Zabisco glared at him and then decided to ignore the insult and answer the question. "I was a little, uh, angry after I heard that she was going around with Thor."

I smiled my most sympathetic smile at him. "Did you say some stuff that you shouldn't have?"

"Yeah, something like that," he conceded. "And stop smirking at me!"

Apparently trying to smile sympathetically at a dog was beyond my talents. I wiped the smile off of my face. "So you just want me to tell her that you're sorry?"

"Yeah."

I could've sat there and asked him some boring professional type detective questions. Questions like where he was on the night that Thor found the bologna or if he had access to liquid fertilizer. The Dog Patrol had probably already covered all of that routine stuff and if I asked nicely, they might provide me with the answers. Doing this favor for Zabisco might lead to something more interesting than standing here talking to him.

"Sure, I'll tell her. Give me a second." I turned to Chuck. "Why don't you go back to my house? Yoshi wanted you to be there when he woke up from his nap."

Chuck didn't have much of a response; he just gave me a nod and then took off towards the front of the house. Apparently watching my mission was too much for Zabisco, so he turned around and went back inside his house. I jumped over the fence and landed in Missy's yard. Missy noticed my intrusion immediately and ran up to me, yapping and snapping all the way.

I stood my ground and tried to not react. She stopped when she got about three feet away. "What are you, crazy? I could tear your head clean off and you just sit there?"

I smiled. "I didn't think that a beautiful, elegant dog like you would soil herself with the likes of me."

She returned the smile and sat down. "What do you want?"

157

"For starters, I have a message for you from the dog next door."

"Really? What is it?"

"He asked me to tell you that he's sorry. He looks like the type of dog who needs that particular message delivered a lot."

She laughed. She had a nice laugh with a musical lilt. "You've got that right. Did he say what he was sorry for?"

"No, I suppose it was a general apology good for whatever bad thing he's done most recently."

She stopped smiling at that. "Anything else? I don't think you come here just to tell me that."

"Do you know Penelope?"

"The cat that lives with Thor?"

"Yeah. She thinks that someone tried to poison Thor."

Her eyes narrowed. "I can believe that."

"Who'd want to hurt a nice dog like him?"

She made a sarcastic dog noise that sounded like "Pssssh!"

"I think that reaction puts you on my list of suspects."

"You do that," She said. "You can make me number one on the list and I'll bet you know why."

"My friend Yoshi would say that he impugned your honor."

"Whatever. I say that he's a lying jerk."

I shivered. "It seems to be getting colder and since all of the ice out here is melting it must be you. So did you soak a slice of lunch meat in poison and serve it to that lying jerk?"

"No, I didn't!" She was outraged. "Now if you don't have any more messages or insults, I have some business to attend to." She walked towards a nearby tree.

"I don't have any more messages, but I'm sure I could come up with a few good-" I stopped talking when she squatted towards the tree. I could take a hint.

It was actually getting warmer. The ice covering the ground was getting thinner, wetter and the grass underneath was poking through. I hopped back over the fence into Thor and Penelope's yard. Penelope was nowhere to be seen but Thor was sitting on the ground next to his house. He was staring intently at something on the ground beside him. I approached him and he must have heard me coming but he didn't look up.

"You still here?" He asked while still staring down to his right.

"Yeah, I'm just basking in the glow of your hospitality. What the Hello Kitty are you looking at?"

I sighed and prepared myself to sit there and wait for who knows what. I didn't have to wait long. The sigh was hardly out of my mouth before a big drop of water fell from above and hit the ground on which Thor had been concentrating.

"Whoa!" he yelled

I couldn't understand what he was getting so excited about. "What are you yelling about?"

"That water keeps dropping on this spot! For no reason! It's not even raining!"

I wasn't sure if he was serious. "Have you tried looking up?"

He looked at me as if I were speaking gibberish. Then he looked up.

"What's that?" he asked.

I gazed up at what he was looking at. There was a big icicle hanging directly over our heads. It was attached to the roof of their house and the warming was making it melt.

"It's called an icicle" I said in the tone of voice that you might use when speaking to a slow witted child.

"I know that!" he exclaimed. "What do you want?"

"Penny thinks that somebody is out to get you and I can help you, believe it or not."

"I don't believe it!" He snorted. "I can take care of myself. Now get out of here before I get mad!"

"You should be mad at whoever put that poison out for you to eat. Don't you even want to know who did that?"

"I don't want some scrawny little orange cat looking out for me. Why don't you go – "He stopped in mid-sentence, distracted by another water drop hitting the ground. He barked at the ground as if the water drop owed him money. He barked so loudly that after he was done my ears were ringing.

After I was sure that I could hear, I asked, "Can you just tell me about that bologna? Where exactly did you find it?"

He looked at me as if I was crazy and then sighed and said, "It was on the back porch. Right there. I came out the doggie door and there was a slice of meat. Man, do I like bologna! Do you know that it was invented back in – "

"Did it seem odd in any way?" I interrupted him.

"Yeah, it smelled weird. Smelled all chemically."

"Why would you eat something that smelled like that?"

This question actually seemed to render him speechless. After he blinked a couple of times he managed to speak. "It was bologna"

We both stopped and thought about that for a second. We only had a second because another water drop landed next to Thor. Of course he barked at it like it was a mortal threat. You would have thought that I'd be deaf at this point but I could barely make out a dog approaching us from the driveway.

"Shut up!" A familiar voice barked. "I'm getting complaints on the noise. From India!" A big brawny German Shepherd came out into view.

His name was Duke and he led the Dog Patrol. They walked around the neighborhood keeping the peace. I usually got along with Duke but Yoshi gave him a major pain and vice versa. Yoshi once told me that Duke's natural authoritarian attitude clashed with most cats' inborn independence. I didn't know about that but neither of them missed an opportunity to get on the other's nerves.

As soon as he came around and saw us I could tell that something was wrong. His head jerked up, his eyes bugged out and he was obviously looking at something alarming directly above Thor and me. I'd known Duke for most of my life and I could count on one paw the number of times I had seen this look on his face. Instantly I realized that there was some kind of danger above our heads most likely related to the icicle we were just talking about.

"Come on!" I shouted and launched myself at Thor's neck. Grabbing his collar in my teeth, I ran away from the house. A cat my size shouldn't have been able to pull a dog Thor's size but he got the idea and ran with me.

SMASH! Something heavy crashed and shattered on the ground that Thor and I had just rapidly departed. I looked back over my shoulder to see a mound of crushed ice. The icicle that had been hanging off the roof had fallen and almost landed right on top of us.

Duke was staring up at the roof. "I could've sworn I saw somebody up there!" he growled. There was an implied order in that statement. Duke wanted me to climb up onto the roof and see if anybody was up there. I didn't particularly care for taking orders from a dog, implied or otherwise but if there was someone up there who had just tried to push a ton of ice down onto my head, I wanted to have a conversation with them.

I jumped onto the fence, leapt from there onto a nearby tree, climbed the tree and then jumped onto the roof. There was nobody there. The snow had melted down leaving just bare roof shingles.

"Well?" Duke called up. I could look down and see him and Thor looking up at me.

"Nothing," I yelled back. "The snow's all gone up here so there's no footprints or tracks."

Duke grunted, "Do you smell anything?"

I closed my eyes put my nose in the air and inhaled deeply. My eyes popped open in shock and my whiskers began to twitch.

Duke's eyes widened. "What? What is it? What do you smell?"

I smiled down at him. "I think I smell your breath. Have you been eating your own poop again?"

"Get back down here!" He was not happy.

By the time I got back down he was in full lecture mode. "Look kid, I know that you like your little jokes but somebody just tried to kill you!"

Thor was shocked. "Kill us? Could that really have killed us?"

"Nah," I disagreed. "It would've just hurt a little."

Duke growled, "Sure, the kind of hurt where they take you to the vet and you come back two days later in a little box that your owners put up on their mantle."

Thor whimpered a little. Duke didn't take his eyes off of me. "Let me guess, Penelope didn't think that the dog patrol was moving fast enough so she went to Yoshi?"

That got a big grin from me. "Not the first time that someone's been dissatisfied with your efforts and come to us."

"Hmm. I was surprised that she didn't call Yoshi in the first place, what with their history and all."

"History? What history do they have?"

Having demonstrated that he knew something that I would like to know, Duke turned to Thor. "You, you're being pretty quiet."

"Yes, sir?" Thor answered.

"I didn't hear you thank this cat for pulling you out from under that ice."

"Pull?" Thor got a little indignant. "He didn't pull me! He kind of tugged on me and I followed. I could have -"

Duke was giving him a hard stare as he spoke. This had an effect on Thor so he stopped what he was saying and just looked at me and said, "Thanks, dude."

"You're welcome."

Duke wasn't done with him. "OK Thor, this seems to be the second time somebody's tried to knock you off. Who is it?"

Thor sat on his haunches, thought for a second and then said, "I don't know. Everybody around here likes me."

He had actually had the nerve to look surprised when Duke snorted and I laughed. "What?"

I turned to Duke. "I don't know about you but I've only been here for a little while and I don't think I've met anybody who didn't want to kill him."

"You have no idea. This boy annoys everybody in the general vicinity. I've had to come up five times to tell him to lay off all the noise and I know the human police have talked to his owner."

"I don't suppose that anybody actually threatened to kill him?"

"Nah. He was irritating but I hadn't heard of anyone going that far."

I thought that I'd push my luck. "While you're in a mood to answer questions, are you absolutely sure that you saw somebody on the roof just now?"

Not considering that worthy of a response, Duke looked at Thor and said, "OK, playtime's over. Who wants you dead? And

I don't want to hear any nonsense about how every loves you. You ain't that stupid."

"I don't know!" Thor said. "I know that there's some guys around here that don't like me but none of them have the guts to mess with me! One time this mastiff came up to me and thought that I was going to back down and I –"

He was interrupted by Duke. "Shut up! How about you just answer the questions I ask you and make it short and sweet, OK?"

"Yes sir."

"Now, tell me exactly what happened when you found that meat? Hey where are you going?"

Duke's first question had been for Thor but his second question was directed to me. I had started walking to the driveway.

"I have to go," I answered. "My humans are out of town and the lady they've got checking on us will be at the house soon."

"You sure you don't want to stick around and help me question this guy?"

"Actually I figured that you could handle it. Maybe afterwards you could drop by and compare notes?"

Duke grimaced. "I haven't seen Yoshi in a couple of months. It would be a pleasure to see him." It's very hard for me to convey how much sarcasm was in his tone. I knew perfectly well that he'd rather have a little kid pull on his tail than go see Yoshi.

"I know you're not eager to see him but I was here for a while this morning. You might want to hear what I've learned."

He looked skeptical. "After you and Yoshi have decided what you should and shouldn't tell me, right?"

I was trotting towards the front of the house. I called back over my shoulder, "OK, we'll see you at our house in a couple of hours."

I'm pretty sure that I heard Duke sigh as I trotted away.

CHAPTER 6

When I got home Chuck and Yoshi were in the dining room, crouched over a book, studying it intently.

"That's an 'F'," Yoshi was saying. "It makes an 'eff' sound. Can you say that?"

"Eff." Chuck repeated.

I walked right up to them. "Learning to read?"

Chuck looked up. "Yep. I'm learning the alphabet!"

"Try to say 'yes' instead of 'yep'," Yoshi corrected him.

I hated to interrupt the kids' English lesson but I forced myself. "Somebody just tried to kill Thor and me. I thought that you might be interested"

Yoshi looked at me thoughtfully. "Interesting. You must have been exceptionally obnoxious. They don't usually try to kill you for a day or two."

"I have a ways to go before that bunch would think that I'm obnoxious. Wait until you meet Thor." I gave him a broad smile. "By the way, Duke will be here in about an hour."

Yoshi sighed. "I was hoping to have a quiet Christmas Eve, not bicker with an over officious canine. Tell me."

"Sure." I answered. But before that, how about we a take a moment to discuss the party? It's not too late for me to put together a Christmas party that they'll talk about for years."

Yoshi didn't say a word; he just gave me a withering stare that made it crystal clear that his position on us throwing a party hadn't changed since yesterday. With that established I sat down and reported the morning's events to Yoshi. He lay down, closed his eyes and looked like he'd fallen asleep. Despite his appearance I knew that he was soaking in my every word. Chuck sat next to him and actually looked like he paying attention to me, which was nice of him since he had already seen most of what I was reporting.

It didn't take me long to relate what had happened. When I was done Yoshi opened his eyes, yawned and sat upright. He usually had a few questions after I gave a report.

"Did Duke actually see someone on that roof?" he asked.

Since I had repeated all of my conversations, Yoshi knew that Duke had stated that he'd seen someone on the roof multiple times. So his real question was whether or not I believed Duke. "This is Duke we're talking about." I replied. "The former police dog. He's a trained observer or at least that's what he always telling me. If Duke says that someone was up there, then someone was up there."

"Hmm. But you yourself didn't see this figure on the roof?" Yoshi was skeptical.

"I admit that I was preoccupied by not getting impaled with a giant icicle but you can ask him yourself. I told him to come over and –"

I stopped talking as I heard footsteps on the front porch. It was Mrs. Murphy, our neighbor from across the street. While our people were away Mrs. Murphy was coming over once a day to fill our food bowls. By the time she entered the house, Yoshi had curled up and was pretending to be asleep, Chuck had run into the living room and hidden himself under the couch and I went up front to greet her. Mrs. Murphy was very efficient. She went straight to the kitchen and filled our food and water bowls. Then she came back up front to pet my head, went to the dining room and found Yoshi and gave him a quick pet. She was gone in five minutes.

After she had left, Yoshi and Chuck went back to work on the alphabet. Apparently we were dropping the Thor business until Duke arrived. That was fine with me. I jumped up on the nearest chair, closed my eyes and took a nap.

I got about an hour and a half of sleep before Duke arrived. Yoshi and Chuck were still in the dining room, crouched over the workbook. I brought Duke in just as Yoshi was going over the usefulness of the letter 'Y'.

"Who's the kid?" Duke asked in a tone of voice that implied that he didn't like the fact that a kitten existed in the neighborhood that he didn't know about.

Yoshi looked up with an annoyed expression. "I wasn't aware that I needed to consult with you about whom I invite into my home."

I could see the fur on Duke's back rise. This was the effect the two of them had on each other. If I didn't interject, they would just pointlessly bicker all afternoon. "Will the two of you relax?" I said. "Duke, this young kitten is named Chuck. You've heard of the something the cat dragged in? I'm the cat and he's the something. I found him last night on the streets and since he had no place to stay, he's going to hang out with us until our people get back from Christmas vacation."

Duke's hard gaze went from me to Yoshi. "You're letting a strange cat stay here? That doesn't sound like you at all. You must have gone soft for the holidays. Or is something else going on?"

Yoshi probably would've delivered a crushing retort if I hadn't jumped in again. "Yes, yes, yes. We're all filled up with the Christmas spirit. So what happened with Thor after I left?"

"A whole lot of nothing. That loudmouth thinks that he's most popular dog in creation, meanwhile everybody he knows wants to cut his throat."

"So Gatsby was telling me," Yoshi murmured. "How far has your investigation gotten?"

Duke sat his big german shepherd body on his haunches. "Apparently not far enough for Penny, since she went to you. Although I don't understand why she didn't go to you in the first place."

"She and I may not have parted on the best of terms. That has no bearing on the matter at hand. Were there any developments over there after Gatsby had to leave?"

Duke snorted. "Nothing that I would call a development. I talked to all of the significant players and got nothing for my efforts. Zabisco and Missy both claim that they were inside their houses when that icicle was knocked down at Thor."

"And you are sure that someone was on that roof above them?" Yoshi asked.

"Yes." Duke said testily. "I know that Gatsby's already told you that. Where are you going?"

Yoshi had stood up, turned and started towards a window a few feet to his right. "Nowhere," he said and then he jumped up onto the windowsill. "I just needed a better view."

"Hmph," Duke snorted. "You just need to look down on me."

"Not at all. I just like to be able to view things from a suitable vantage point."

Duke wasn't buying it. "I think that you just do stuff like that to remind me that cats can climb and jump to places that dogs can't."

"Absurd! Don't let your jealousy of me distort your view of my behavior–." Yoshi stopped in mid-sentence. For a second he looked as though he was about to say something but then he shut his mouth and just stared into space.

Duke and I knew enough to leave Yoshi alone but Chuck couldn't keep quiet. "What's he doing?"

"Hush!" I whispered. "He's thinking. Why don't you go play?"

"Play with what?"

"This is a big house. There's plenty of stuff to amuse you. Now shoo!"

Chuck trotted out through the door. I turned back to Yoshi, who was showing signs of life.

Yoshi blinked a couple of times and it seemed safe to ask him a question. "OK, so who did it?"

"Who did what?" He answered testily.

"Who poisoned the bologna and then tried to dump that ice on Thor and me? I saw you go into think mode just now so I know you know."

Yoshi sighed. "I'm not quite there yet. There are a few points that Duke may be able to help clear up?"

"Sure," Duke said. "What do you need?"

Yoshi raised his eye whiskers and looked at me. I smirked back at him. Then we both looked at Duke. Yoshi said, "You seem very cooperative. Gatsby, do you remember what Duke said the last time I had questions for him in a matter that we were both investigating?"

"I believe that he told us to go lick ourselves and then he gave us a lecture on interfering with dog policework."

Duke wasn't amused. "What were these points that you wanted to clear up?"

Yoshi sighed. "Unfortunately I'm not sure. I have formulated a theory as to what is going on. However since we've only been on the case for such a short time, I'm afraid that there may be gaps in my knowledge that would derail my interpretation of events."

"You don't know what you don't know." Duke said.

"Precisely. But if I'm going to make an accusation, I'd like to know as much as possible. You've been at this longer than we have. Can you give us a quick overview of your investigation?"

"Sure. I'll start at the beginning. Penelope called me a week ago and told me about Thor. He found a slice of bologna in his backyard that smelled funny but he wolfed it down anyway. He got violently ill and had to go the vet and get his stomach pumped. His housemate Penelope asked me to look into things. She'd been back in town for a couple of weeks and neither she nor Thor claimed to have any idea who would want to kill him. I asked around the neighborhood and the most likely suspects were the human neighbors due to his habit of violating local noise ordinances."

"He did what?" I asked.

"You know, disturbing the peace. I must've been out there to tell him to shut up at least once a week."

Yoshi was beginning to get bored. His tone was flat as he asked, "So you think that a human gave him the bologna?"

"I did at first. Then he told me that there were teeth marks in the bologna."

"Indeed?" Any trace of boredom had vanished from Yoshi's voice. He shot me a quizzical look.

"Penelope didn't say a word to me about teeth marks." I said.

Duke smirked. "She doesn't know about them. I found out about them when I questioned Thor in detail. He'd forgotten about them until I directly asked him if there were teeth marks on the bologna."

I had a question. "What kind of teeth marks? Cat? Dog? Platypus?"

"He didn't know. He was sure that they were animal teeth marks but he had no idea what animal they came from. Even after the meat made him sick, he was proud of himself for having taking the meat that some other dog or cat must've lost."

Yoshi thought about that for a second. "Do you mean to tell me that he found a piece of lunchmeat in his backyard that had a strange smell and had teeth marks on it and he ate it?"

"Yep." Duke replied. "He's a character. Of course the important point about that is that if there were actually teeth marks, then an animal must have left that meat there for Thor. I'm going to have a talk with Zabisco about that when I get back over there."

Yoshi wasn't saying anything so I asked another question. "So you think that it was Zabisco?"

"Look kid, it was either Zabisco or Missy. They had a classic love triangle going on. Toss in a long lost twin brother and a fire at the orphanage and the humans could make it into a TV show. Those two are the animals with the deepest grudge against Thor. What was that?"

That last question referred to a rustling sound that we heard coming from elsewhere in the house, probably the living room.

"It's just Chuck." I answered, "He won't hurt you, he just –" I stopped talking as I realized that Yoshi was deep in thought again.

Duke noticed too. "Does he have it figured out now?"

Yoshi wasn't that far gone. "Not quite," he answered.

"Well what have you got?"

Yoshi frowned. "I've got it by the tail. I have a theory but I don't have enough information to prove it to my satisfaction or yours. I need you to get those animals here so that I can speak with them but I doubt that you'd be willing."

"Right you are. I'm not your errand boy. I don't think that you've got anything – you just want them here so that you can fish around and see what you can dreg up. You can do it without me."

"Even if it means that our would-be killer gets more time to make another attempt on Thor's life? Regardless I can't send Gatsby to bring them here. Since they don't believe or care that someone is trying to kill Thor I don't have sufficient inducement to get them to come. I need them here tonight!"

A lightbulb turned on over my head. "I have a suggestion."

The smile on my face was all the clue Yoshi needed to tell exactly what I had in mind. "Absolutely not!"

"Oh come on! It will get them here and it'll give you a big audience for when you explain whatever's going on."

Duke was confused. "What are you two talking about?"

Yoshi ignored him. "It would actually serve another purpose as well. Very well. You can have your party."

"Yes!" I shouted.

"But you'd better make sure that this house is immaculate afterwards."

"Of course."

"You can start by picking up the Christmas tree and putting the ornaments back in place."

"Why would I have to pick up the Christmas tree?" I asked and was immediately answered by the sound of a crash in the living room.

I dashed through the doorway with Duke right on my heels. He almost crashed into me when I stopped short just inside the room. The Christmas tree was down, a mass of twisted branches and tinsel surrounded by ornaments on the floor in front of the fireplace. Chuck's little head poked out from the middle of the tree. "It was so big and pretty. I couldn't resist trying to climb it."

"Geez," Duke muttered. "Somebody must've overdosed on cute pills this morning."

"Yeah," I agreed. "Now Duke, if you want an invite to the party of the year, please help me pick up this tree."

CHAPTER 7

You would think that I would have to scramble like I had rabies in order to get a party put together for that very night. Fortunately I had assumed all along that I would be able to talk Yoshi into the party and made arrangements accordingly. A couple of days ago, I had invited all of the animals in the neighborhood to a Christmas Eve get together at my house. I had also arranged the food, music and everything else that makes for a good party.

There had been a couple of alterations to my plans as Yoshi had come up with a couple of special preparations. The most significant task was hanging a curtain between the kitchen and the dining room. If you're wondering how Chuck, Duke and I managed to mount a curtain, I'll just say that it wasn't easy.

Everything was taken care of by seven o'clock that night. Chuck and I sat at the back door in the kitchen waiting for things to begin.

Chuck was visibly excited. "I thought that the party didn't start until eight."

"When did you learn how to tell time?"

"Yoshi showed me a few things this afternoon when you went out with Duke."

I stared at him stupidly for a few seconds. If Yoshi had been working with Chuck when I went out, it meant that he had skipped his afternoon nap. Inconceivable.

I snapped out of it and said, "The reason I went out was to invite a few animals to the party a little early. Hopefully they'll be here in a minute."

"Is it Thor and those cats and dogs we talked to this morning?"

"Yep. Yoshi wants to have a chat with them before the party."

"Is it so that he can figure out who's trying to kill Thor?"

That made me chuckle. "No, he already knows that. We have to prove it and do something about it. That's going to be the tough part."

"He already knows?"

"Sure. So do Duke and I." I smiled at his blank stare. "It's not hard to figure out. You'll know too if you think about it for a second."

He had yet another cute moment as he squinted his little eyes and went into a state of deep thought.

"You can think later." I told him. "Sounds like our first guests are arriving."

I had heard a couple of animals approaching. Thor was the first to enter in from the doggy door, followed by Penelope.

"Hey!" Thor barked out in his booming voice. "I'm here! The party can start!"

"Sure," I replied. "How was the walk over?"

"It was fine!" Thor was back to his normal talkative self. "It's getting cold though. I can smell a storm coming tonight. You remember that blizzard two years ago? I smelled that one coming. I tried to tell my man and you know what he said to me?"

"No!" I said while I had the chance. "Why don't you save that story for the party? I'm depending on you to delight the crowd with you dazzling small talk skills."

While he tried to figure out just how sarcastic I was being, I turned to Penelope. Her eyes locked onto mine as if she had been waiting for years to get my attention. Just as she was about to open her mouth to say something, I realized that I was only going to get one chance to do something truly hilarious.

"Where's Yoshi?" She and I both said simultaneously.

Penelope frowned while Chuck and Thor laughed.

"I'm sorry," I said. "I'm just playing with you. Yoshi will see you all in a minute. He wants to talk to you all in a group before the party."

That seemed to take Thor by surprise. "What group?"

As if to answer his question Zabisco came in followed by Morris the cat and then Missy. Neither Zabisco nor Thor seemed pleased to see one another. They both eyed one another without saying a word which must've been torture for Thor.

As much as I liked to see uncomfortable dogs, I had a plan that I needed to follow now that everyone was in attendance. "OK, I asked you guys to get here a little early so that my colleague Yoshi can have a chat with you before the party. But he's not quite ready for you yet. So why don't I give you a tour of the house and then I'll take you to see Yoshi."

Nobody seemed happy about that development but nobody complained and they all followed me. Chuck was beside me in the lead with Thor a couple of feet behind us. Then came Penny and Missy with Zabisco and Morris bringing up the rear.

First I showed them the garage which was accessible through another kitchen door. Our family had taken the car so there was nothing in the garage but old paint cans, a small jug of paint remover and some gardening implements. I explained that we were keeping the door to the garage open to make sure that the house didn't get overheated. Surprisingly no one seemed to care. From there I took them upstairs to see the kids' bedrooms and the master bedroom (or Yoshi's office). We then went back downstairs and went through the living room where no one seemed impressed by the Christmas tree. From there we went through down the hall to the dining room and then doubled back and wound up back in the kitchen.

I had been noting their faces and attitudes during the tour and I hadn't seen anything of much interest. Thor had kept interrupting with stories about how much bigger and better his house was. Everyone else was quiet although Morris kept yawning every few minutes.

When we entered the kitchen through the living room there were two things that were immediately noticeable. One was that we had to go through the curtain that I mentioned earlier. I explained that the curtain had been hung to keep the party goers away from the food until we were ready to serve it. The second noticeable thing was the food. Lined up against the kitchen wall just beyond the curtain were twenty bowls in two rows filled with every pet food and treat that I could get my hands on. In addition to regular garden variety cat and dog food in both dry and wet varieties, there was also beef jerky, salmon bits and rawhide bones. There was even some raw meat (don't ask me where I got that).This impressed them. Thor in particular was staring hungrily at the beef jerky.

I didn't want Thor getting his hopes up. "Hey Thor, Penelope told me about your dietary restrictions. That bowl was made especially for you." I nodded my head towards a stainless steel bowl that contained one cup of dry dog food.

"Really? That's it?" There was a palpable disappointment in his tone then he looked back and gave Penelope a fearsome glare.

Yoshi's voice rang out. "Right now, your health is our primary concern."

Yoshi was up on the kitchen counter looking down on us. Beneath him was Duke, sitting on the floor and looking annoyed.

"Hello Yoshi." Penelope mewed.

"Hello Penelope." Yoshi replied with a smoothness in his voice that I don't think I'd ever heard before. "You and I will have to catch up during the party. But for now, I'd like to speak with you all."

Missy wasn't pleased. "I came here for a party, not to be interrogated."

Duke fixed his gaze on her. "The party's still on. We just want to talk to you guys a little. Now you all know about the allegedly poisoned bologna that Thor ingested –"

He was interrupted by a grunt from Yoshi.

"I'm sorry," Duke said, not sounding sorry in the least. "Do you want to do this?"

"If you don't mind. This is my house and we are working on a case that you couldn't handle until my arrival."

"Couldn't handle!" The fur at the back of Duke's neck was standing up at full attention. "Listen to me, you arrogant little –"

I was going to say something before the two of them really got going but before I could say a word, Penelope jumped in. "I can't believe that the two of you still act this way after all of these years. Duke this is Yoshi's house. Why don't you let him speak? If he says something that you don't like, you'll be right here."

Duke gave her a short nod. Yoshi addressed the group. "As you all know Thor ingested a slice of lunch meat that someone poisoned. His housemate Penelope contacted Duke as she was afraid that there might be another attempt on Thor's life. When she was unsatisfied with Duke's performance, she decided to get someone competent and contacted Gatsby and myself."

Duke let that one pass. His left eye twitched but he didn't say a word.

Yoshi continued. "You all met Gatsby this morning. You probably also know that shortly after Gatsby spoke to all of you someone made another attempt on Thor's life. Thanks to Duke's alertness and Gatsby's reflexes that attempt also failed. However it was very suggestive in that – yes? Do you have something to say?"

That question was directed to Missy who had made a snorting noise. She looked startled at being addressed but snapped right back to her normal haughty state. "No. I don't have anything to say."

Yoshi eyed her coolly. "That's a shame. I asked you all here early in the hope that you would have something to say. As the animals that know Thor best I thought that you four might have an insight as to who is trying to harm him."

He paused for a couple of seconds to let that sink in and then continued. "I'd rather not sit here and fire questions at you so I'm going to invite each of you to speak. I'd like you to just share any information that you might have that would be relevant to this situation. Zabisco?"

Zabisco hadn't expected to be called on first. "What?"

"What do you know about these attempts on Thor's life?"

Zabisco just scowled. After a few seconds I yelled, "Speak boy! Speak!"

All of the dogs in the room gave me dirty looks.

Yoshi sighed. "Please ignore Gatsby. When he was a kitten someone told him that he was funny and now he feels the constant need to prove it." Having dealt with me, he turned back to Zabisco. "Well, what have you got to say?"

"Nothing." Zabisco growled.

"Ah well. Perhaps someone else will be more talkative. Penelope?"

"No, wait." Zabisco must have changed his mind. "I do have something to say."

He paused for a second, then licked his lips and continued. "I don't know who's trying to kill Thor and if I did, I'd yell at them for the punk job they're doing."

He shot Thor a glare and Thor glared right back at him.

"I just want to tell Missy that I'm sorry."

This statement provoked three separate reactions: Yoshi sighed, Duke grunted and Missy said "Really?" slightly less haughtily than she normally spoke.

"Yeah. I should've known better than to believe anything he says."

Missy gave him a little smile and said, "Its ok."

Chuck whispered to me. "What's going on? Why isn't she mad at him anymore?"

"I think it's the Christmas decorations." I answered. "They seem to make everybody more forgiving."

Chuck and I weren't the only ones commenting on the proceedings. Thor, definitely not whispering said to Penelope, "He's acting like a little she-pup. I wonder if the humans had him neutered this afternoon."

A switch in Zabisco's brain flipped to 'savage'. A low, throaty growl came from behind his teeth and then his body sprang at Thor. He didn't make it. Thor backed up until his butt was against the refrigerator and Missy stepped between the two of them. Zabisco tried to push past Missy but Duke came up, clamped his teeth on Zabisco's collar and dragged him back a few feet.

Thor sat back and barked loudly and unintelligibly at Zabisco. I couldn't understand what he was saying and listening hurt my ears. Zabisco also contributed to the noise pollution in the kitchen by alternately barking at Duke to release him and then telling Thor what he was going to do to him when he was released.

Yoshi had had enough. "Silence!" he hissed. "It's bad enough that there's going to be a party here tonight, I won't have my house turned into a coliseum!"

For whatever reason that shut Thor and Zabisco up. Zabisco calmed himself enough that Duke let go of his collar.

Yoshi waited until he was sure that everyone was looking up at him. "If we can resume? Zabisco's contribution to our discussion was irrelevant and almost led to violence. Perhaps we can do better. Missy do you have anything to contribute?"

She wasn't shaken at all. She coolly answered, "I didn't find it irrelevant at all. I thought it was sweet. Sorry if our lives inconvenience you. I don't know anything about who's trying to kill that one and that's all I have to say."

"Fine." Yoshi said dismissively. It was time to move to someone else.

Since Penelope had presumable already told me whatever she had to say, Morris was the only one left to call on and he knew it. He was wearing his customary smirk and looked like he was ready to speak.

Yoshi obliged him. "Morris, what about you? Do you have anything to say on this subject?"

Morris was wearing his customary smirk. "I told Gatsby everything I know. Besides I think we just got a demonstration from the dog who most wants Thor dead."

If he was hoping to spark a reaction, he was disappointed. After the dust-up between Zabisco and Thor nobody was going to get too worked up about Morris's accusations.

So that was it. If the object of this exercise had been for Yoshi to unearth some buried bit of information that would point to the culprit, it had failed. Fortunately that hadn't been the purpose at all.

The meeting was over. I'm pretty sure that Yoshi was thinking of a way to wrap it up but he didn't have to bother. We heard paw steps approaching from outside and then the doggie door opened and in came Molasses, my favorite cat.

Like any good party guest Molasses had brought something. She had a full brown paper bag in her mouth that she dropped when she saw the gathering in the kitchen. "I thought that I was a little early. Has the party started?"

"No," Yoshi said. "But it may as well. We're done here."

With that he jumped down off the counter and he and Duke left through the doorway to the living room.

After they had departed everyone looked at me. I flashed them my most winning smile and said, "You heard the cat. Time to start the party!"

CHAPTER 8

A half hour later the party was in full swing. We welcomed close to thirty dogs and cats from around the neighborhood. It was a good turnout but lower than I'd expected. A lot of the neighborhood pets simply couldn't leave their homes on Christmas Eve without being missed. Out of the four members of Duke's dog patrol, only Duke was able to attend as his owner had to work that night.

Another factor keeping potential party goers away was the weather. As animals arrived all they could talk about was how the temperature had dropped, how fast the snow had started to come down or how windy it was getting. The general consensus was that the party had better be worth it because everyone was going to have to fight their way through four foot high snow banks to get back to their homes.

A lot of the guests had brought treats with them. Molasses' bag had been full of Shrimp Scampi that her owners had brought back from a four star restaurant. Others brought catnip, bones or even dead mice. Since I was providing food for the party, most of the treats that the guests brought were used as stakes in the party games.

We had stairway races in which Solomon the Siamese, widely known as the fastest cat in the neighborhood, took on all challengers. There was a game of 'pin the nose on the human' going on in the living room and some cats were in the basement seeing who could spit the furthest.

We also had music. In the dining room, two tabby brothers, Teddy and Leo sang a sweet rendition of "Everybody Wants to Be a Cat" just to annoy the dogs in attendance. After they were done Thor got in front of the Christmas tree and belted out "The Cat Came Back" in his deep loud baritone. He really seemed to relish the parts of the song where the cat was being tortured and he downplayed the parts where the cat comes back. This amused the dogs and drew hisses from the cats. It was all in the spirit of fun and nobody's fur got ruffled. Literally.

With that many cats and dogs of all sizes and dispositions under one roof, I had fully expected that there would be insults, arguments and maybe even a little violence. There was none of that on this night. Everyone was being weirdly nice to one another. Even Percy, the dog who had chased me the other night, came up to Chuck, Molasses and me and actually apologized. Although we could hear the wind and snow beating against the outside of the house, there was plenty of warmth on the inside.

About an hour after the party started Yoshi came trotting down the stairs. He had been in the master bedroom taking a regularly scheduled nap. Anybody who wasn't Yoshi might have thought that it was bad form to take a nap while you're hosting a party, especially if you suspect that one of the attendees is trying to murder another one of the attendees. Yoshi was never one to let trifles like that interfere with his sleep. When he got to the bottom of the staircase, he shot me a look. I was on the other side of the living room at the doorway leading into the kitchen. I responded by shaking my head.

He didn't get a chance to come over and talk to me as Penelope picked that moment to swoop down on him and start talking. I couldn't hear what she was saying but Yoshi sat down and engaged in conversation with her although I knew that he wanted to ask me how everything was going.

I checked the clock. It was 9:00. It had been half an hour since I'd heard from either Chuck, who was posted in the kitchen or Duke, who was patrolling the house. It was getting late and I was starting to worry that I was going to spend the entire night watching the curtain that we'd hung between the living room and the kitchen.

As I was thinking about my misspent evening, Molasses approached me. "Hey handsome, where's the mistletoe?"

I cocked my head at her. "Mistletoe? That stuff is toxic."

She rolled her eyes at me. "I don't want to eat it, silly! What's going on?"

"What do you mean?" I asked innocently.

"You know what I mean. You boys throw a party and Yoshi goes off to take a nap and you haven't left this room all night. Yoshi's behavior is normal for him but yours needs explanation."

"This room is party central. I need to stay in here to maintain proper control of the party atmosphere."

"You need to spend time with me and not this curtain." She eyed the curtain. "Why'd you guys hang this thing here, anyway? It looks weird."

"Yoshi's been getting into interior decorating," I lied. "He says that the curtain helps the dining room flow better."

She wasn't buying it. "What's really going on? I know when you're up to something."

"Shh!" I whispered. "I'm working."

"Oh!' her eyes widened. "What is it? That thing with Thor?"

"Shhh!" I repeated as apparently the first time didn't take.

"OK, fine. Be mysterious. I'm just going to stay here and talk to you. You'll look suspicious sitting here all night by yourself."

"It can't be any more suspicious that you telling me that I'm going to look suspicious."

At that point Chuck came into the room. He came in from the hall and he looked worried. He also forgot to give me the signal that we'd agreed on but the look on his face was enough to tell me that something was up. Duke came in about a second and a half later. He made sure that he caught my eye, then he gave me and quick nod, turned around and headed back to the hall.

Duke's nod set off a ten second timer in both of our heads. I turned back to Molasses. "Can you see if you can quietly get everybody's attention on me? You've got seven seconds."

She didn't even question me, she just started going up to guests, head-butting them and nodding towards me.

I had jumped up on the end table next to the couch which was close to the kitchen doorway and the curtain that hung there. When the countdown in my head was close to ending, I took a quick look around the room. Molasses had done a great job in seven seconds and there were a lot of eyes looking at me.

I gave Molasses a wink. Then I turned and leapt off of the table. I grabbed the top of the curtain with my mouth and then gravity took over and both the curtain and I dropped to the floor. Duke turned on the kitchen lights from the dining room entrance. With the curtain down, everyone in the dining room could see into the kitchen where the food dishes were sitting. Right in the middle of the bowls was Morris the cat. He had the handle of the jug of paint remover from the garage in his mouth and he was pouring it into the food bowl that had been designated for Thor.

I called out to the crowd: "Ladies and Gentlepets, here is our entertainment for tonight: Morris the murderous cat!"

The jug dropped out of his mouth and hit the floor. He glared at me. "So this was just a cheap trick!" He hissed.

"Yeah," I replied. "But it wasn't my idea."

Yoshi had jumped up on the end table from which I had just leapt. He smiled. "The cheap trick, as you call it was my idea. I knew that you were the culprit but I needed you to make it clear."

Morris had recovered his composure by this point. "And how did you know that? I thought that I was being pretty careful."

The house was quiet. All you could hear was the wind and snow beating against the outside of the house. There were at least thirty animals in the living room that had been partying it up a second ago but were now silent and listening to Morris and Yoshi.

"Not careful enough." Yoshi said. "You tipped your paw when you tried to collapse that icicle onto Thor. If you were trying to keep suspicion on Zabisco or Missy that was absurd. There's no way a dog could climb up onto the roof of that house. A cat could easily manage it. And the only cat with a reason to want Thor dead is you."

Thor, who had been uncharacteristically quiet asked, "What reason? Why does he want to kill me?"

Yoshi told Morris, "Well, You want to tell him?"

Morris grimaced. "You're so smart. You tell him."

"Very well. I will. But I think that it might sound a little more sympathetic coming from you. I'm afraid that you're going to need all the sympathy you can get."

Morris didn't say a word. He just sat there in the middle of the food bowls with his smirk, not looking the least bit like someone deserving of sympathy.

Yoshi didn't take his eyes off of Morris but he seemed to be addressing everyone in the room. "My perception of your motivation is that you have normal feline needs that were being frustrated by Thor's behavior and personality."

Word must have gotten around the house that something was going on in the living room. All of the party attendees were now in the living room and hanging on every word. Duke had gone through the kitchen and was now sitting a couple of feet behind Morris.

Yoshi continued. "All of the cats among you know that an adult cat requires sixteen hours of sleep each day."

I shouted out a question. "Then why do you insist on twenty-three?"

Yoshi gave me a withering glare and then continued. "About seventy-five percent of this sleep is a light sleep from which the cat can awaken suddenly. This helps cats in the wild get their rest while also being aware of predators and prey. The remainder of a cat's sleep is a deep sleep wherein a cat will dream and may not be aware of noises."

"So what?" Thor was a little angry. "This little freak's been trying to kill me and you're talking about cats sleeping?"

"Shut up!" Duke growled. It was a low growl that was about one hundredth of the volume of Thor's normal speaking voice but somehow Duke commanded more attention.

"OK," Thor said and sat on his haunches.

Morris turned to face Duke. "Oh now you tell him to shut up! How many times did you get called over to get him quiet? How many times did the human police get called? And he never shut up!"

Gears were turning inside Duke's head. "Wait a minute. You mean that this is because he couldn't get all of his catnaps?"

"Catnaps?" Morris yelled, "I couldn't sleep at all!"

Yoshi smiled at him. "I understand. I don't know what I'd do if I couldn't get my required daily allotment of sleep."

"You'd do exactly what I did." Morris had lost his cool demeanor and was getting excited. "You can't imagine what it's like! Every time I closed my eyes I would hear him! He yells at the mailman! He argues with Zabisco about their stupid romances! He'll ask you what time it is and if you don't know, he'll tell about his uncle that was a watchdog at the clock factory and how he stopped a robbery! He never shuts up and he never turns down the volume!"

Nobody had anything to say to that. For a few seconds all that could be heard was the sound of the weather outside.

Of course the silence was broken by Thor. "Wait a minute! I'm not the bad guy here; he's trying to kill me! It reminds of that time those chipmunks took a shot at me."

"I thought I told you to shut up!" Duke roared.

Thor immediately shut his trap. After Duke was satisfied that Thor was going to keep quiet, he spoke to Yoshi. "He does have a point. I can't have pets trying to kill other pets in my neighborhood."

Some voices in the crowd began murmuring. I heard someone comment that Thor had it coming. Someone else said, "That poor cat!"

Duke addressed the crowd. "Look everybody, we are housepets. We can't go around killing each other like feral animals! Even a feral animal only kills for a good reason. Killing somebody because they're disturbing your beauty sleep sounds like something a human would do. Morris needs to be punished!"

That quieted the crowd but Yoshi wasn't impressed. "What exactly are you suggesting?" he asked in a cool tone.

"He should be banished. I want him to get out of this house right now and then get out of my neighborhood. If I ever see him again, I'll rip him to shreds!"

Banishment was the most extreme form of punishment that Duke could impose. For a pet, to be exiled from your home was the most horrible thing that could happen to you. It seemed kind of harsh for an incompetent murderer like Morris. Another gust of wind rattled the windows as I spoke. "This doesn't seem like a really good night for a banishment."

"Hmpf!" Duke snorted. "Was this a good afternoon to get your skull split by a falling icicle? Because that's what almost happened!"

I didn't have much to say to that. Yoshi on the other hand did have something to say. He looked out at the crowd and said, "The holiday that the humans celebrate tomorrow exists to commemorate the birth of a great man. A man who advocated forgiveness among the many things he taught. In view of the fact that Morris didn't succeed in his goal perhaps we can be a little forgiving."

This set off protests from the dogs in the room. Duke spoke for them. "So, you're saying we should just let him walk because it's Christmas? So he can go home and try to kill Thor again?"

Yoshi smiled. "Not quite. I'd suggest something along the lines of what the humans would call probation."

Duke sighed. "OK. Spit it out. What exactly do you have in mind?"

"I'd like to offer Morris some forgiveness in exchange for a favor."

Morris had been silent and very worried looking. He looked up and grasped at whatever straw Yoshi was offering. "What favor?"

Yoshi ignored him and looked at Penelope. "Does Morris have a good home?"

She thought about for a second then said, "Better than he deserves. It's a nice family. A single mom and two little girls in a big house. They're great. The girls want to play but Morris usually hisses and snaps at them.

Morris got a little defensive. "Lack of sleep can make you a little mean."

Yoshi was sympathetic. "No doubt. Morris, I want you to bring home a kitten. You'll get your family to take him into your home as a new pet. He will report back to me frequently and if he reports any further misbehavior on your part, you will be banished as Duke suggests."

Chuck had walked up to Yoshi's end table and looked up at him. "Am I the kitten?"

"Yes. What do you think?"

"Could I still hang out with you and Gatsby?"

"Absolutely. I insist on it. We have a lot to do to continue your education. Will you do it?"

"Sure." Chuck didn't seem to be thrilled to be going to live with Morris but it would have to be better than the streets.

"Wait a minute," Duke had something to say. "You had this all worked out, huh? You talk about showing forgiveness but I notice that you're also getting your little stray friend a home."

Yoshi answered him in the same tone of voice that you'd use on an annoying kitten. "Do you object to this arrangement?"

Duke actually smiled. "Nah. But I want the kid to report to me as well. Not only do I want to know what Morris is up to but I also want to know if there are any further violations of the local noise ordinances. And there better not be!"

He was staring at Thor as he spoke. Thor didn't say a word. Neither did Morris.

"Well Morris?" Yoshi said. "Can you get Chuck established in your home?"

"Yeah, it shouldn't be a problem. I suppose it's better than getting banished."

"Yes it is. I'm going to want to see Chuck almost every day. You will facilitate that. Also I want to make something very clear: if Chuck seems to be being intimidated or if any kind of harm befalls him then you will look back on this night and wish you had been thrown out into that blizzard."

"That's right!" Duke and I said in unison.

"I said its ok!" Morris growled.

Yoshi turned his attention to Thor. "What about you? Do you have a problem with this arrangement?"

Duke answered for him. "He's fine with it!"

Thor kept quiet.

"So that's it," I said. "The case of the poisonous cat. What a weird Christmas story."

Chuck looked up at me. "What is the story with Christmas?"

"What do you mean?"

"What is Christmas all about? I don't get it but it seems pretty important. Can you explain it? You and Yoshi are the smartest cats I've ever met." He said all this while he stared up at me with his big, cute kitten eyes.

I didn't have the slightest idea of what to say. I looked around. Molasses was smiling at us like this was the cutest thing she'd ever seen. Yoshi and Duke were sitting next to one another smirking and barely containing their laughter. The two of them didn't agree on much but seeing me in a tough spot seemed to bring them together. I was about to say something to change the subject when Yoshi put in his two cents. "By all means, Gatsby tell all of us the Christmas story," He said in a raised voice that carried through the house. "Everyone, Gatsby is going to tell us all about Christmas!"

Everyone in the room waited for me to speak. I realized that this was Yoshi's payback to me for us having had a Christmas party. Whatever. I had seen enough Christmas specials that I knew what I needed to know about Christmas. I licked my lips and addressed Chuck, but in a loud enough voice that everyone could hear. "Well Chuck, a long time ago, a baby was born in Bethlehem."

"Where's that?' Duke yelled, in an obvious attempt to trip me up.

"Its in Pennsylvania, you dope!" I yelled back. "And stop interrupting! I'm talking to Chuck!" I looked around. Everybody looked quiet and attentive. I looked back at Chuck. "Now, as I was saying a baby was born in Bethlehem. His name was Christ and he had super powers. When he got a little older, he got a pet reindeer named Rudolph that had a really bright red nose that fired heat blasts and he was friends with a snowman named Frosty who had a magic hat that enabled him to come to life and um, gave him super strength."

I took a second to look around. Everybody was quiet and paying attention. This was going much better than I could have anticipated. Yoshi and Duke were still looking like they were about to crack up. I went on. "So the baby was awesome and he and his friends used their powers to help people. So the people celebrated his birthday every year and called it Christmas."

"Oh, this is good!" Duke barked.

I heard Yoshi whisper, "Hush! He's on a roll!"

Ignoring their rudeness I continued, "There were two people who were jealous of the baby and wanted to destroy Christmas, their names were um, Scrooge and Potter and they were the worst kinds of human villains: bankers. So they foreclosed on all of the people's houses and had their henchman, the Grinch steal all of the Christmas stuff. Christ and his team knew that they had to stop the bad guys, so they had the Ghosts of Christmas Past, Present and Future use their time travelling powers to show Scrooge what life would be like if hadn't existed. This got him to betray Potter and talk the Grinch into becoming a good guy. Potter went to jail. The Grinch was still wanted by the cops for all of his stealing so he changed his name to Santa Claus and to make amends instead of breaking into houses and stealing people's stuff, he now breaks in and gives out gifts to kids every year at Christmas. The end."

I looked around. Everyone was looking at me, not making a sound. Chuck looked at me and said, "That was great!"

The room began filling with chatter. I heard comments like, "That totally makes sense." And "Yeah, that's the story alright. That's the same way my mother used to tell me."

Duke still looked amused. Next to him Yoshi looked like he was about to cough up a five ton hairball. He had assumed that I was going to make a fool out of myself but there actually were times that things didn't go as he planned. "Hold on!" He shouted, "Are you all rabid? That was the most ridiculous thing I've ever heard!"

"That's my story," I said, "and I'm sticking to it."

"You got something better?" Duke asked Yoshi.
Yoshi jumped up on the coffee table where a Bible was conveniently located. He pawed open the book and shuffled

through the pages until he found what he was looking for. There was still some chatter in the room when Duke barked, "Everybody, shut up and pay attention to the cat!"

I shook my head. Duke was quieting a room for Yoshi. That was a Christmas miracle in and of itself. Duke's command was followed and about thirty pairs of animal eyes were on Yoshi.

Yoshi sat atop the coffee table with the book open in front of him and the Christmas tree all lit up behind him. "Here is the real Christmas story," He began, "I'm going to alternate between the books of Matthew and Luke. I'll start with Luke 1:26 – God sent the angel Gabriel to Nazereth, a village in Galilee to a virgin named Mary. She was engaged to a man named Joseph, a descendant of King David. Gabriel appeared to her and said, 'Greetings, favored woman! The Lord is with you!'"

He kept reading and everyone was hanging on every word. Except for Yoshi's voice, everything was quiet except for the sound of the wind and snow beating against the house. Molasses snuggled up next to me and gave me a couple of nose licks. "What a wonderful night," She said. "Merry Christmas."

I returned the nose licks and said, "Merry Christmas to you too."

I looked around. The clock said that it was midnight. There were about thirty cats and dogs listening raptly to what Yoshi was reading. Penny was looking at Yoshi with what I took to be admiration. I wondered if that was going to lead to anything.

I suppose that there are miracles all around if you look hard enough. Chuck was lying in front of me. He was purring lightly and was going to have the first good night of sleep he may have ever had knowing that soon he would be off the streets and in a real home. Thor was over by the Christmas tree and was actually quiet. Quiet. He wasn't talking or yelling or barking. He was just listening to what Yoshi was saying. Everything was looking great.

At least until tomorrow when I'd have to clean up the house before our people came back.

THE END

PETECTIVES: UNDER FIRE

Robert J. Smith

"Cats are a mysterious kind of folk – there is more passing in their minds than we are aware of."

Sir Walter Scott

CHAPTER 1

It was a late morning in early July and it was hot. Horribly, ridiculously hot. As I walked through my neighborhood on my way to a ten o' clock appointment, I was mentally cursing the humans for the whole global warming thing. I usually loved to be outside but on that day I couldn't wait to get back to my air conditioned home. The humans that I lived with usually turned the AC down before they left for work and daycare but the temperature in the house was still cooler than what I was dealing with outside. The sidewalks were so hot that I had to walk across the lawns so as to not burn my paws and when I got to a driveway or had to cross a street, I raced across as fast as possible. Fortunately my appointment was only a few blocks away from my house.

The neighborhood showed all of the signs of a protracted heat wave. It was easy to tell which houses were obeying the water restrictions by how brown their grass had become. Even though school was out, there weren't many kids outside. In fact there weren't many people outside at all as apparently most of them had enough sense to stay inside when the temperature hit three digits.

Not being blessed with that much sense, I trotted on to my destination. My partner Yoshi had reacted with shock and horror when I'd told him that I had to go out to meet a potential client. He was of the opinion that any cat that would willingly go outside in this weather was out of his mind. To look at him you might assume that the reason for this attitude was the fact that he was a black cat and everyone knows that the color black absorbs heat. That might be a good theory but it wouldn't explain why he refused to step foot outside of our house at any other time of the year.

If the color of your fur determined your level of comfort in extreme heat then a lightly striped orange cat like me should be fine but I was feeling the heat as much as anyone else. The sooner this meeting was over with the better.

When I got close to the street corner that served as the location of my appointment I got the first of several nasty surprises that I was going to receive over the next couple of days. There were three dogs sitting at the corner, a big German Shepherd, a medium sized Bulldog and a small but formidable looking Pit Bull. The German Shepherd's name was Duke and he was the leader of a four dog organization that provided a form of law enforcement to the neighborhood animals. The Pit Bull was young and friendly looking (for a Pit Bull). His name was Rocco (a.k.a Rocky) and he was a member of the Dog Patrol. He didn't take things quite as seriously as Duke, but then I've met junkyard dogs with toothaches that were less serious than Duke.

The Bulldog's name was Percy and he was something of a neighborhood bully. He was typically kept chained in his backyard where he would threaten and intimidate any animals in the vicinity. The few times that he had gotten loose, he had chased some animals around but he had never hurt anyone. He was the prototypical dog whose bark was worse than his bite. One of the pleasures of my life was sitting just beyond the reach of Percy's chain and mocking him. There's nothing better than getting a dog all worked up into a frenzy but unable to do anything about it.

This situation was very odd. Normally the way my life worked was very simple. Most of the time I ate, drank and slept the days away. Then occasionally someone who needed the kind of help that Yoshi and I could provide would contact me, usually through a messenger like Murray the mouse. Last night Murray had told me that someone wanted to consult me but that it was extremely confidential and that he wouldn't tell me who it was. I had no problem with those conditions but usually under these circumstances I would meet a female cat who would want me to follow her significant other and see if he was tomcatting around. It looked like today I was here to meet two dog cops and a bully.

I had slowed my pace a little to consider what might be happening. Duke noticed and in a growl that I could hear from a block away said, "Hey Gatsby, don't slow down. We won't hurt you."

I gave a loud exaggerated sigh and quickened my pace. As I approached the dogs I said, "Yesterday Yoshi said something like only mad dogs and Englishmen would go out in heat like this. Where's the British guys?"

Duke grunted. "You're hilarious as always."

"Sorry. You guys surprised me. I was expecting a damsel in distress."

Duke nodded his head towards Percy. "He's your damsel in distress."

I laughed. Percy opened his mouth to protest but a sharp glare from Duke shut him up.

If we were going to have this meeting it had better be out of the sun. "Look, whatever it is you boys want me for, can we discuss it in the shade?"

There was a gigantic pine tree in the front yard of the house nearest to us. I headed for the shade that it provided and the three dogs followed me. I sat with my back to the tree trunk and the dogs all sat facing me.

Percy spoke first. "Look, I ain't a damsel —"

"Shut Up!" Duke barked. "I'll let you know when you can talk."

Percy shut up. It was a pleasure to see him have to take being ordered around. He could be pretty nasty to the cats and smaller dogs in the area but he wasn't about to challenge Duke.

Duke turned back to me. "Look kid, we need your help. Percy's got a problem."

"Percy's got several problems," I said before Duke could get another word out. "His looks, his personality and we can't forget his smell."

That got no reaction out of Percy. Three of them just stared at me. "Are you done?" Duke asked.

"Sure. Go ahead."

"Percy's been accused of attacking another dog."

That raised my eye whiskers. "Really? You finally went after somebody?"

"No!" Percy said, "It wasn't me."

Since Percy was always yelling about the unspeakable acts of violence that he was going to commit if he ever got loose from his chain, I already believed that he had attacked whoever had accused him. However since he was sitting here with Duke and Rocco and not cooling his paws at the Animal Control facility probably meant that things weren't that simple. "So what happened?"

Duke reported in his matter of fact tone. "Two days ago at approximately 3:35 pm Sophie, the Pomeranian who lives next door to Percy was attacked in her front yard by a dog. Sophie is positive that Percy was her assailant but no humans witnessed the incident."

"She survived?" I asked.

"Yes," Duke replied. "She was cut up and bruised pretty badly but her attacker ran off and her owners discovered her on their front lawn and rushed her to the vet. She got stitched up and is currently in the vet's office over on Brice road. I was able to have a quick chat with her last night."

"OK. What's Percy's story?"

Percy spoke up. "I was chained up in my backyard like I am everyday. I heard the commotion but it was up front so I couldn't see what was going on. I didn't even know what happened until Sophie's people came to my house and yelled at my owner about it."

"Why would they yell at your owner?" I asked. "Duke just said that there were no witnesses. I'm pretty sure that Sophie couldn't tell the humans that you jumped her."

Duke got back into the conversation. "Percy's attitude and reputation make him the obvious suspect when an incident like this occurs."

"Yeah, I'll bet" I said with a grin.

Percy wasn't grinning. "I heard the lady next door say something about taking me away and putting me down."

That seemed unlikely if no human had actually seen anything but I wasn't about to offer any kind of comfort to Percy.

Rocco picked that moment to speak. "Duke, you haven't told the cat what we need him for."

Duke replied in a very patient tone of voice. "I shouldn't have to. He's gotten enough information to figure it out. He likes to make deductions and stuff like that." He looked at me. "Isn't that right kid?"

"You've got me and Yoshi mixed up. He's the one that deduces. I wouldn't make deductions if animals had to pay income tax. I can however make wild guesses based on practically nothing and sometimes be correct. Let me try. Since you and Rocco are here with Percy, I'm going to assume that you don't think that he did it. Since Duke emphasized that there were no human witnesses to this incident I'm going to assume that there was an animal witness or witnesses. And since Duke has come to me and he doesn't usually want Yoshi or me within a thousand miles of any case he's working on, I can assume that the witness isn't being cooperative with the Dog Patrol but might talk to me. So I'm guessing that this witness is a cat and that you want me to talk to him or her. How did I do?"

Rocco looked pretty annoyed with my guesswork. "You did great. Too great. Who's your source? Is somebody telling you Dog Patrol business?"

Duke sighed. "Settle down Rocky." Then he turned to me. "Rocky doesn't know you as well as I do. You were correct in your guesses or deductions or whatever you want to call it."

"Induction." I said.

"What?"

"I think that the technical term for what I just did is induction." I replied.

"Whatever!" Duke barked, "I don't have time for your nonsense. I would've gone straight to Yoshi but he's a bigger pain than you are."

I smiled. "Heat getting to you?"

"Yeah and as usual your attitude isn't helping. A cat that lives in that area has been telling everybody that she saw Percy attack Sophie. When I tried to talk to her she clammed up. There's another cat that lives directly across the street from Sophie and who is known to constantly sit in his front window. If he was in his window yesterday, he wouldn't have been able to help seeing exactly what happened but he claims that he didn't happen to be in his window at that particular time."

"And you think he's lying?"

"He didn't seem exactly forthcoming when I talked to him."

This was great. Usually a frequent hazard of my chosen profession was a very long boring speech from Duke about how Yoshi and I shouldn't be interfering in Dog Patrol business. Now here he was practically begging for our help. Yoshi was going to love hearing about this. "So would you like me to have a chat with these cats?"

Duke grunted. "Sure, but I want Yoshi to talk to them too."

"Fine," I said. "But I usually have a better way with the ladies."

Percy burst in with, "Just let Yoshi do this!" Percy had always held Yoshi in high regard.

"You guys do what you think is best." Duke said.

"Fine." I said. "So what is it you're trying to achieve here? You can't actually think that Percy might be innocent?"

Duke gave Percy a sideways glance. "I know that the humans probably won't get enough evidence to do anything but if I find out that Percy here mauled a pet I will personally kick him out of this neighborhood!"

This was too much for Percy. "I told you I didn't do it!" he whined.

"Shut up!" Duke responded. Then he turned to Rocco. "Keep an eye on Percy. I need to talk to the cat alone."

Duke looked me straight in the eye and walked over to the hedges. I followed him wondering what else he wanted.

"Look kid, I had a talk with your girlfriend yesterday."

"Molasses?"

"Yeah."

"What did she need from you?"

"Well she didn't want me to tell you but I thought that I'd better."

"Okay," I said. My powers of induction had left me. I had no idea what he was talking about.

"She told me that she's gotten a visit from our old friend, Nails."

I could suddenly feel my heart beating in my chest. "That nasty pit bull we put away last Halloween? She escaped from Animal Control?"

"Apparently. She has two dogs accompanying her. Molasses said that Nails demanded food under the threat of violence. After Molasses fed them, Nails told her that they would be back."

"This was yesterday?"

"Yep. She didn't want me to tell you because she was afraid that you'd do something stupid. Don't prove her right."

CHAPTER 2

I made a beeline for Molasses' house. She lived a few blocks away and by the time I had gotten there I had cooled off. Well, figuratively at least.

The heat certainly hadn't died down. I was looking forward to getting to Molasses' house and getting inside. Her people had left town on vacation a couple of days ago and had left her behind in a big house with the air conditioning on. Hopefully I could cool down in the house while she explained to me why she hadn't told me about her nasty visitor.

There was a white male cat panting on the front porch of Molasses' house. His name was Butterscotch and he lived with Molasses. I had been on the top of his enemies list ever since Molasses had made it clear that she preferred me as a boyfriend and him as a friend friend.

"Hey Butterscotch," I called to him. "Is it hot enough for you?"

He made a face like you make when you've lapped up some milk without sniffing it and then realize that it's spoiled. "What kind of idiotic question that? It's unbearably hot! Why would you ask that?"

"Just making small talk."

A feminine voice spoke from behind me. "Don't mind him. He's just grumpy from the weather."

It was the love of my life, Molasses. She was a big white cat with a few black patches. Although I always thought that she looked hot, today that was taking on a different meaning. The heat didn't seem to be affecting her as much as it was Butterscotch but she did seem to be panting slightly when she said, "Hey Sexy. What's up?"

When I turned to face her, the smile that had been on her face vanished. "What are you mad about?" she asked.

She knew me better than anyone besides Yoshi but I can't say that I cared too much for her being able to read me like that. Especially when I thought that I was wearing a cheerful expression on my face.

"I'm not mad about anything," I protested.

"Yes you are. You look too happy, you're obviously trying to hide anger!"

Butterscotch had a good laugh at this. I shot him a glare. He just smirked back at me, got up and strolled off to his backyard.

After he was gone, Molasses continued with her questioning. "Well?"

"I told you that I'm not mad."

"Oh, please. I know you better than you know yourself."

"Fine," I conceded. "Then you should know why I'm mad."

She looked at me for a second and then her eyes narrowed. "Duke! He told you! He promised that he wouldn't tell you!"

"Well, he's known me since I was a kitten. So when he finds out that my girl is being threatened by a dangerous thug who has said that she's going to get violent bloody revenge on me, he feels like it's something that he should tell me. He's weird that way."

"Hmph."

That wasn't good. The last time that she said "Hmph" like that it was followed by two weeks of her giving me the silent treatment.

"OK," I said. "Whether you wanted me to know or not, I know. When did you see her?"

She sighed. "Nails came by yesterday morning. She barked until I came out to talk to her."

"What did she want?"

"She said that she was new in the neighborhood and that she needed help."

"Help?"

"She was very nice about it, but she said in so many words that something bad would happen to my house if I didn't get her food every day."

"She said that?"

"Yes. Not in those words. She said it in a nice, non-threatening way but that's exactly what she was saying."

I thought for a second. "So she's running a protection racket in our neighborhood? Duke must be choking on his dog biscuits."

"What's a protection racket?" Despite having hung out with me for the past several months, Molasses was still a bit naïve when it came to crime.

"It's from human gangsters. Usually some tough guys go to some small business owner and tell him that they will prevent vandals from smashing his windows or wrecking his property if he pays up. If he doesn't pay these same guys are the ones who do the smashing and wrecking."

"That's terrible!" she gasped. "Have you seen this happen before?"

"Well not in person." I admitted. "But I've seen it on TV. So did she have anything else to say?"

"Well she knew that my people are gone on vacation until next week. And she told me not to say anything to the Dog Patrol. Or to you and Yoshi."

"Really?"

"Yes, really. And I know what's going through your little orange head. You're thinking 'she couldn't wait to go tell Duke but she wasn't going to say a word to me!' Isn't that right?"

I shrugged. "I guess so. We've already established how well you know me."

"Well I don't want you trying to fight a pit bull! She almost killed us last Halloween!"

"Hmph!" I grunted.

She opened her mouth to respond but then stopped and tilted her head as she'd heard something and was trying to hear it better.

I heard it too. There were three dogs approaching from the west. I turned my head and into view came my old friend Nails the pit bull. She was followed by two other mean looking dogs.

They were proving how tough they were by walking on the scalding hot sidewalk without showing any sign of being the slightest bit uncomfortable. Nails was just as ugly as the last time I saw her with her scarred face clenched into a glare. I didn't know the two dogs that accompanied her, one was a black Doberman the other a dopey looking brown Boxer with a white belly. They both had angry looks on their faces but they had a long way to go before they could match the intensity and meanness displayed on Nail's face.

Molasses wasn't visibly frightened. "I don't suppose that you'd be open to running away and not getting yourself killed?"

I gave her a grin "Well, you know me better than I know myself. What do you think?"

She just sighed. I stepped up so that I was between her and the approaching dogs.

The dogs didn't seem relieved at all as they stepped out of the hot sun and into the shade of the tree that Molasses and I were sitting under.

I gave them a cordial greeting. "Hey Nails. What's up?"

She didn't return my friendliness. "The last time I saw you I told you that I was going to rip your head off and then reach into your neck and pull your heart out."

"Oh. Is that what you were saying? It was hard to make out what you were talking about from outside that animal control van. How is it that you're not enjoying the hospitality of our local animal control facility?"

She smirked. "I didn't like that place. So I left."

There had to be a lot more to the story than that but I wasn't interested. "OK. So now you're back and running a protection racket. Welcome back!"

She looked confused for a split second. "Protection racket? What's that?"

"It's where you warn that something bad is going to happen to someone unless they pay you to protect them. In reality you're the one that will cause the something bad that the someone would have to be protected from."

Nails' smirk broadened into a smile. "That's interesting. What's it got to do with me?"

I smiled back. "I've heard that you and your crew were demanding food in exchange for your assurance that bad things won't happen."

Nails looked at the Doberman to her right. "Hey Fusco, do you know what he's talking about?"

The Doberman shook his head. Nails looked to her left at the Boxer. "How about you Geech?"

Geech shook his head and said, "Naw. I wonder who's been telling stories about us?" He was staring past me and directly at Molasses.

"Doesn't matter." I said. "Since Nails here is a known professional criminal, she has the credibility of a street rat."

"Whatever." Nails' smile vanished. "Me and the boys here are just letting it be known that we're available to solve any problems that come up. No different than you and that black cat. No different than that idiot German Shepherd and his Dog Patrol."

"Except that we don't cause the problems." I shot back.

"None of this matters to you anyway."

"On the contrary, this matters to me a lot. I take a deep interest in the affairs of my neighborhood. I believe that it's my civic duty to –"

"Shut up!" Nails interrupted, "What I meant was that none of this matters to you because me and my boys are about to rip you from limb to limb."

"Ah."

"Get him!" she ordered.

CHAPTER 3

This was not a good situation. There was a tree behind Molasses and me but the dogs would be all over me before I could turn around and climb it. It looked like the best I could hope for was to hold off the dogs long enough for Molasses to escape.

"What's going on here?" A low voice rumbled from behind the dogs.

It was Rocky the Dog Patrol Pit Bull with whom I had just conferred. Either he had followed me without me noticing or he had just showed up at the right time. Either way he was the first and hopefully the last dog that I ever had the urge to kiss.

"Who are you?" Nails barked.

"My name's Rocco. I'm with the Dog Patrol. Who are you?"

Nails responded with a word that I'd rather not repeat here. The dogs had stopped advancing on Molasses and me.

Molasses whispered. "Let's go!"

I nodded and she ran up the tree expecting me to follow. I stayed put. I wasn't about to take off and leave Rocky to deal with the three dogs by himself.

The dogs ignored Molasses. Rocky had the full attention of Nails and her boys. "You're one of Duke's punks!" Nails snarled.

Rocky had walked around the three dogs and took a position standing next to me. "I can see that you dogs don't have licenses, you don't belong in this neighborhood and it looked like you were threatening these cats."

Fusco the Doberman growled, "What are you going to do about it?"

Nails looked annoyed at her underling. "Shut up! I do the talking!"

With Fusco properly put in his place, she turned back to Rocky. "Look, we're just visiting in this neighborhood. I saw Gatsby over here and I wanted to say 'Hi'."

I have to admit that I was actually rendered speechless. Molasses had situated herself on a tree branch directly above us and I heard her snort in disgust.

Rocky wasn't buying it. "Really? Well now that you've gotten reacquainted maybe you could answer a couple of questions for me."

"Do you mean questions like, 'Who are you?', 'Where are you from?' and 'How long are you planning to be in my neighborhood?'"

"Yeah." Rocky replied. He was staring a hole into Nails. The smile had left her face a while ago and she was returning the stare.

If any humans were driving by at that moment we would have made a weird sight. Nails and Rocky were locked into an intense Pit Bull staring contest, neither of them showing any sign that they noticed the heat. In contrast Geech and Fusco were definitely feeling the heat. They were visibly uncomfortable with their panting the only noise that could be heard other than distant traffic.

I was looking as cool as a cucumber sitting next to Rocky and Molasses was looking down on all of us from her perch in the tree. We probably made a lovely tableau for a summer morning.

Nails broke the silence. "I don't have time to answer dumb questions. We're out."

She turned and walked toward the sidewalk. Geech gave us a grunt and followed his boss. Fusco tried to snarl at us but his panting got in the way so he sort of gasped at us and then trotted after the other two. They took the sidewalk and headed north.

Rocco didn't follow them. He just stood there glaring at them.

After the dogs were out of sight Molasses jumped down from the tree. "Thank you! Thank you!" she gushed to Rocky, "I don't know what would've happened if you hadn't come along!"

"No problem. I'm glad that I was here."

That brought up a point that interested me. "How exactly did that happen? Were you following me?"

"Gatsby!" Molasses wasn't pleased with me. "You should be thanking him for saving our lives!"

"Thanks." I told Rocky. "Now, were you following me?"

"You're welcome." Rocky said, "And I didn't have to follow you. Duke knew where you were headed and asked me to come here and keep you from getting hurt."

"Did he? I can take care of myself!"

An arrogant smile spread across his Pit Bull face. "Yeah you looked like you were doing pretty good. Maybe I should call them back and you can show me how you can take of yourself."

I smiled back at him. "That's probably a better idea than you think." Turning to Molasses I asked, "What do you think Duke will say when he finds out that a member of his Dog Patrol let those guys walk off without even following them to see what they're up to?"

Molasses frowned. "He won't be happy, that's for sure. He might even –"

She stopped talking because Rocco was leaving. He took off in the direction that Nails and her goons had gone with his nose to the ground.

"I gotta go," I told Molasses. "If you or Butterscotch see those dogs again you let me know. Where is Butterscotch?"

"I don't know. He probably went inside as soon as soon as those dogs showed up. Do you have to go?"

"Yeah, I have to let Yoshi know what's going on. Remember what I said. If those dogs come around here again, you come get me."

"Sure." She didn't sound very convincing and she looked downright mopey.

I gave her a smile. "I'll be back later."

That didn't seem to cheer her up any.

*****

I got home at about a quarter past noon. I could feel a sharp distinction between the heat of the outside and the coolness of the air conditioned house and I had a definite preference. I found Yoshi in the living room. He was sitting in between two open books.

"You don't read enough of those things?" I asked, "Now you have to take them two at a time?"

He looked up. "I'm making a comparison. One of these books is A People's History of the United States by Howard Zinn, the other is A History of the American People by Paul Johnson. Each book views the history of our country through completely different ideological viewpoints. At this time of year a comparison seemed appropriate. I wish I could get my paws on a copy of Thaddeus Russell's A Renegade History of the United States."

"Sounds fascinating." I lied. Then I let loose with a loud yawn that I stretched out to last about ten seconds. "Sorry about that. It's been a while since my last nap."

He sighed. "It hasn't been that long. Do you have something to report? I hope that your meeting was worth going out into that inferno outdoors."

"You have no idea. Percy's been accused of mauling another animal but Duke doesn't think that he did it. Also Nails the Pit Bull is back and she's offering protection to some of the neighborhood animals. She went to see Molasses first."

"Ah."

That seemed like an odd reaction. "Ah what?"

"You seemed a bit agitated. Now I see why. Is Molasses ok?"

"Yes, she's fine. Do you want the works?"

Yoshi sighed and lay down. "Yes, it sounds like I need a full report. Proceed."

Before I could start a visitor arrived. Another cat strolled into the room. His name was Chuck and he was lucky enough to look a lot like me only he was smaller and not quite as orange. I had met him last Christmas when he was a stray kitten and Percy was chasing him through the streets. I rescued him from Percy and then he stayed with us until Yoshi found him a home. Chuck visited us a couple of times a week to get educated. Yoshi taught him junk like reading and math while I showed him valuable things like how to follow an animal without letting them catch your scent or how to get specific information out of a suspect without letting them know what you're after.

After we'd exchanged greetings, Yoshi told him, "Sit down. I may have a new case. Gatsby was just about to report."

"A case?" Chuck was excited, "Can I help?"

"No!" Yoshi and I said simultaneously.

"Sorry kid," I apologized, "But you're still a little wet behind the ears."

"Whatever." He sighed. Typical adolescent reaction. He took a seat.

I also sat down and delivered my report. Thoroughly describing everything that had happened from my meeting with Percy, Duke and Rocco through what had happened at Molasses' house took about half an hour.

Chuck listened attentively to every word I spoke. Yoshi on the other hand looked like he had drifted off into a deep catnap, which was how he usually listened to my reports. I did notice that his eyes opened a crack when I described my encounter with Nails and her friends. Shockingly, by the time I'd finished his eyes were wide open and he was sitting upright.

"Any questions?" I asked.

"Just one. How long are Molasses and Butterscotch's people going to be out of town?"

"Uh, they left for Disneyland yesterday and they're coming back five days from now."

"Who's feeding the cats?"

"The woman who lives next door to them comes twice a day to fill their bowls. So what?"

"So nothing. I was just curious. Never mind. I believe that you'd better go talk to the witnesses Duke mentioned."

"Now?" I admit that I may have been a little whiny. "I wanted to get a nap! I haven't slept all day."

"Fine." Yoshi always hated to interfere with any cat's sleep. "You get some rest. It can wait until later."

Chuck had other ideas. "If Gatsby's too tired, I could go talk to those cats."

Yoshi gave him a withering look. "I thought that we'd made it clear that your assistance wouldn't be necessary."

Chuck had nothing to say to that.

"You know," I said, "Duke and Percy were pretty insistent that you speak with these cats."

A quick scowl formed on Yoshi's face. "Duke does not dictate how you and I conduct ourselves. We are not official members of his Dog Patrol." He took a second to shudder at that thought. "We will operate us usual. You will talk to these cats, examine the area where this incident took place and report back to me. Then we will decide if I need to talk to these witnesses."

"Okay." I replied. Then I enjoyed a nice yawn.

Yoshi looked at Chuck. "Let's get on with your studies. Can you tell me the three stages of Hegel's dialectic?"

Even though Chuck's lesson for today was sure to put me asleep immediately, I decided to take my nap upstairs in one of the kids' bedrooms.

I went up the stairs, entered the girl's bedroom and jumped up onto her bed. After spending about ten minutes cleaning myself I was ready for sleep. I glanced out of the window and got a surprise. From my position the window looked directly out onto our front yard and the houses across the street. I saw Chuck walking away from our house. That seemed odd as Yoshi's lectures could go on for hours. Maybe Chuck had failed his homework so badly that Yoshi had sent him packing. I wasn't in the mood to care too much. I just shut my eyes and drifted off.

CHAPTER 4

I woke up at about 3:00 refreshed and ready to get back out. But first I wanted to talk to Yoshi. I found him on the living room couch just waking up from his own nap.

"Wakey, wakey!" I called, "I don't want you sleeping too long. You don't want to be late for your next nap."

I had to wait for a response until he had finished a long yawn. "Amusing," he said. "Aren't you going out?"

"Yeah but I had to ask you something first."

"Yes?"

"Right before I drifted off I would've sworn that I saw Chuck leaving which made no sense since he had just gotten here. Was I dreaming that?"

"No. As usual you saw correctly. I had an errand for him."

"An errand?" I said in a tone of mock annoyance. "I thought that I ran the errands around here. Is that kid taking over my job?"

"Don't be silly. You had to have your nap so I used Chuck."

"Was it to interview those witnesses about the Percy situation?"

"No. But now that you mention it –"

"I'm going, I'm going!" I walked to the doorway and then stopped and sniffed at the air.

"Well?" Yoshi demanded.

"I thought that I got a faint whiff of Duke." I explained. "Was he here while I was upstairs?"

"If he had been here while you were asleep, wouldn't you be getting more than a faint whiff?"

"Yeah, but–"

"I suggest that you get a move on."

Something was wrong. On the one paw he was right. If Duke had been in the house, his scent would be a lot stronger than I was detecting. On the other paw, he didn't come right out and say no. On the third paw, Yoshi would often do things involving our cases and not let me know until he absolutely had to. I'm not sure why he did this but I think it was to show me that he wasn't entirely dependent on me to gather information. Whenever I questioned this, he would say that a cat was sometimes compelled to be mysterious. That seemed reasonable if he was talking about relations to dogs or people but not between him and me. On the fourth paw, I didn't really have anything for the fourth paw.

"Well?" He said. "I don't blame you if you're forestalling having to go out in that dreadful heat but if you're going, you might as well be on your way."

I didn't have a response for that so I did as he suggested.

*****

When I got to Percy's house it was a little after 3:30 and the heat hadn't died down a bit. I went to the backyard to see Percy but he wasn't there. You could usually count on him being chained to his back porch most of the day but either he was still out with Duke or his people had actually let him inside the house. There was nothing in the yard but scorched grass and the empty chain. I went back to the front of the house and then crossed the street to approach the house directly across from Percy's. It was a two story off-white structure with black shutters on all of the windows. I trotted up the stairs onto the porch. There was a white cat lying in the front window behind a screen. I wouldn't say that he was fat but it was a safe bet that his vet had told his people to put him on dietary cat food.

"Hi there," I called to him. "My name's Gatsby and I —"

"Ooh! I know who you are! Wait there! I'll be right back!" He disappeared.

I jumped up on one of the two chairs that were sitting on the porch and took a seat. He wasn't gone long and when he returned there was a small cloth bag in his mouth. He put the bag down on the windowsill and used his teeth to pull the cinch on the end of the back to open it. Three plastic figurines fell out of the bag. One was an orange cat in a sitting position, one was a black cat in mid-stride and one was a German Shepherd standing regally.

"I know all about you and Yoshi," he said. "These are my action figures of you guys. My boy used to have action figures of his heroes and I wanted some too. I got these from my girl's dollhouse playset."

Apparently Yoshi and I had a fan. "That's great," I told him. "Although if that black cat is supposed to be Yoshi, he should be laying down. Yoshi's more suited for an inaction figure."

He seemed a little disappointed by my reaction. "I know it's kind of silly but you guys are heroes to some of us."

I gave him a smile. "Don't get me wrong. I'm very flattered. So you obviously know who I am but I don't think that you and I have ever met."

"My name's Willy. I usually stay right here in my window watching the world go by."

"Really? How do you get your people to leave a window open on a hot day like this? I'd think that they would want to keep all the windows shut to keep in the air conditioning."

He laughed. "Ha! They know to leave this window open or I'll throw a fit. I let them close it in the winter but I'll still be here, watching what's going on."

"Your view seems restricted to what's going on across the street. Speaking of which I need to ask you about an incident that you may have seen happen a couple of days ago."

"Are you talking about what happened to Sophie?"

"Yep. What do you know about it?"

"Nothing." Willy's smile and any trace of friendliness vanished.

"But you just said that you're in this window all of the time. You must have seen something."

"No," He replied. "I must have been at my food dish when that happened."

"Maybe you were at your litter box," I suggested. "Because what you're trying to tell me smells like –"

"Hey! Look, I swear that I didn't see a thing. Duke didn't believe me either. Did he send to you talk to me?"

"Well he asked that Yoshi and I might have a word with you. He thought that you might be more comfortable talking with other cats.

"Hmpf! I'm fine talking to dogs. I even have an action figure of him!"

Not wanting to go back to his action figures, I tried to focus the discussion back on the matter at hand. "So what you're saying is that you sit in the window all day and all night but the one time that something interesting happens you just happen to be eating?"

"Yes," he said tersely. "I can't help it if that's how it happened. I don't know why you're asking about it anyway. Is it so hard to believe that that loudmouthed bulldog finally attacked somebody?"

"Well Duke seems to think so and if you have an action figure of him, you must not think that he's a complete idiot."

Willy cocked his head. "Duke's great. But he can still be wrong."

There didn't seem to be much further to go with that line of questioning so I decided to change topics. "Let's forget Percy for a minute. Have you seen three stray dogs around here threatening animals?"

His eyes widened and he sat up. "Yeah! That's why I thought you were here in the first place. I knew you and Yoshi wouldn't stand for this in our neighborhood."

"Of course not," I reassured him. "Tell me exactly what happened."

"Yesterday this ugly pit bull and her friends came up on the porch, right where you're sitting and told me to give her some food from my fridge or she'd burn down my house!"

"She actually said that she'd burn down your house?"

"Well no, not in those exact words. It was more like she said that houses catch on fire a lot when it gets this hot and it would be a shame if something like that was to happen to my house. However if I got her some turkey, then I would be protected from accidents like that."

I smiled. "She's saying that she can control the weather?"

"She's so cocky, she probably thinks that she can. Although I think that she was saying that she might set my house on fire."

"Thanks for clarifying."

"They've been hitting up every pet in the neighborhood. I knew it wouldn't be long before you and Yoshi stepped in and put them down!"

As much as I was enjoying having a fan, it was time to wrap up this interview. "Duke told me that there was another cat around here that might have seen the attack on Sophie."

"Oh, you mean Sunshine. She's been telling all the other cats that she saw Percy attack Sophie but she's not what you would call a reliable witness."

"Why is that?"

Willy smiled as if enjoying a private joke and said, "You'll find out. She lives right next door. She's probably in her backyard tending to her garden."

I jumped down from the chair. "OK, thanks. Would you be available to come to my house and talk to Yoshi tomorrow?"

At first he was excited. "Wow! I get to meet Yoshi!" Then doubt crept in. "I don't know, I don't really leave my house."

"Well, Yoshi absolutely won't leave our house so I don't know how else you're ever going to meet him. You do want to meet the other cat that you have an action figure of, don't you?"

"I guess I could come. I haven't been out of my house in years."

"That's perfect," I said. "You and Yoshi can compare notes on being pathetic shut-ins"

I told Willy how to get to my house and that I'd see him there tomorrow at 3:00. After I descended the front stairs, I headed for the backyard. There was no fence between Willy's house and

the house to the right so I walked right into the neighbor's yard.
If you could call it a yard. Half of it was grass but the half near
Willy's house was filled in by an elaborate garden. There were
rows of plants, some of which were surprisingly green
considering the weather that we'd been having. Between the
rows of vegetation were black hoses which I assumed were there
to provide regular watering. The grassy half of the lawn was also
green and healthy as opposed to the front lawn which I'd
noticed was as dried out and yellowed as the other lawns in the
neighborhood.

Before I'd taken three steps into the yard, I heard some
rustling and a small figure emerged from the garden. It was a
very cute female tortoiseshell cat and she didn't look happy.

"Hey man! Get out of my yard!" She appeared angry but that
didn't make her any less cute. She was sporting a cool tie dyed
collar that contrasted nicely with her brown-black fur.

I gave her my winning smile. "Sorry but I am definitely not a
man. I smell way better."

"Figure of speech, man. I mean cat. What do you want?"

"My name's Gatsby. I just want to talk to you for a couple of minutes."

"Oh, you're that cat detective." She said in the same tone of voice that she would've used to describe a trip to the vet. She probably didn't have an action figure of me.

I kept my smile in place. "There was an incident in the neighborhood a couple of days ago. I wanted to ask you about it."

"Oh, you mean when Percy jumped Sophie." She seemed relieved.

"That's what I'm trying to figure out"

"There's nothing to figure out, man. I saw the whole thing."

I started to tell her to stop calling me 'man' but what was the use? A lot of pets pick their speech patterns from their people and hers were obviously deeply ingrained. "Can you tell me what happened?"

"Sure! I was back here messing around in my garden when I heard a big commotion up front. I ran up there and Percy just

275

had his teeth dug into poor Sophie! He was just tossing her around. It was horrible!"

"What time was this?"

"I don't know. I don't exactly wear a watch."

"Do you know what set Percy off?

"No, I didn't get there until he had already started attacking. But you know that he was always barking and threatening anybody that came within fifty feet of him. It's a wonder that this hasn't happened before now."

This certainly was not new information to me but I decided to act as though it was to see if I could get any more information. "You say that Percy would threaten people? What kinds of threats?"

"Oh don't play dumb with me. I've seen you making fun of him from just beyond the range of his chain! You know perfectly well the kinds of things he would say to any animal that got near his house!"

It was annoying that she knew me that well and I'd never heard of her. "Do you have any ideas as to how he got off of his chain?"

"No, I don't know anything about that. I just saw him tearing into poor Sophie. Poor kid."

There didn't seem to be much to say to that so I shifted to another subject. "Did you say earlier that you had a garden?"

Her face brightened. "Yeah man, I like to get my paws dirty. I plant my own seeds and take care of my plants. Those are my flowers in back."

The plants that she nodded towards were at the rear of the garden area. Most of it looked like regular garden variety vegetation to me. Although some plants stood out from the others. There was one weird plant that was much greener than the others. It had leaves with sawtooth edges and a bunch of purple and white flowers.

Standing around admiring the greenery wasn't going to get me anywhere with Percy's case. It didn't look like Sunshine was going to tell me much more about the incident so it was time to wrap up. "Hey, could you come by my house and talk to Yoshi about all of this?"

She rolled her eyes. "Look, I don't know anything more than what I told you. I'm not going anywhere."

"Oh come on. Don't you want to be one of the few pets in the neighborhood to actually meet Yoshi? He never steps foot outside of our house."

"Yeah, I am kind of curious. I heard that he actually died a few months ago and you've been pretending that he's still around."

"What? Why would I do that? Never mind, why don't you come and see for yourself?"

She sighed. "Fine. I'll go see him. Why not? It might look bad for me if I don't, right?"

"I don't think that anything could make a cute kitty like you look bad. Could you show up at my place tomorrow at half past noon? We're in that big white house on Mercy Street."

She rolled her eyes when I made the "cute kitty" comment but she nodded at the other two sentences so I turned around and took a couple of steps towards the front of the house. I realized that I'd forgotten something and turned back.

"Hey, one more question."

Her eyes widened a little. "What?"

"Have you seen an ugly pit bull around here? Maybe with two ugly friends?"

She gulped. "Yeah, Ive seen them. Are you after them too?"

"Maybe. Did they talk to you? What did they say?"

"That pit bull and her buddies came here yesterday and told me that if I didn't get them something to drink that they would throw me a beating."

"Really? What did you say?"

She shrugged. "I turned the hose on and let them drink."

"They say anything else?"

"Oh, yeah. She told me that I was going to make sure that she and her friends didn't get thirsty or bad things might start happening."

"What kinds of bad things?"

She actually shuddered. "She said that my house may burn down or that my garden could get destroyed if she and her friends weren't looking out for me."

"And all you have to do in return is provide water on demand?"

"Yeah, I don't need the trouble. I told them that they could help themselves."

Duke was going to be furious when he found out the full extent of what was going on. This was the exact kind of situation that he had set up the Dog Patrol to prevent.

"Man, I hate pit bulls!" Sunshine growled.

I would've thought that any cat wearing a tie dye collar would be more open minded. "Well I don't care much for Nails either, but I wouldn't blame her entire species. I happen to know that she was raised by human criminals and I would bet one of my nine lives that she was treated pretty badly."

She snorted. "So that makes it okay for her to take her problems out on us?"

"No, but knowing what her problems are can help us deal with her."

She rolled her eyes again. I didn't have anything else to say so I turned to go. Then something hit me like a ton of cat litter. The mind is a weird thing. My mind is anyway. Back when I had been thinking of how furious Duke was going to be, I was reminded that I had caught a whiff of Duke's scent in my house before I left. That made me wonder why he would've been in my house. When I saw Chuck leave before I fell asleep, he could've been going to get Duke. But why would Yoshi have wanted to see Duke? While Sunshine stared at me I stood there sorting through my memories of this morning, trying to think of what might have spurred Yoshi to send Chuck out to get Duke. And why was it so urgent that he couldn't wait for me to take a nap? Although he wouldn't have sent me even if I hadn't taken a nap

— he had wanted me to go talk to the witnesses, not go get Duke. Was it something that might get me into trouble? Maybe something I'd seen or heard had tipped Yoshi off as to where Nails and her gang were hanging out. But why wouldn't he have told me or sent me to get Duke? Sometimes Yoshi is deliberately mysterious but this seemed absurd. I couldn't believe that he'd have something worth keeping from me that early in an investigation unless it had something to do with me personally. But what aspect of this involved me personally?

"Molasses!" I said.

"What?" Sunshine was confused. "Molasses what?"

"Never mind!" I was on the move. "I'll see you tomorrow at 3:30!"

"OK!" she replied to my rapidly departing backside.

CHAPTER 5

I raced to Molasses' house as fast as four paws could carry me. My mind was racing faster than my paws. It was all coming together. Nails had to be staying somewhere. I had just heard how she was taking care of food and water; shelter would be next on the list of basic needs. Molasses and Butterscotch's people were gone to Disneyland for the week so their house would be a fine place to stay. Yoshi probably guessed all this and then asked Duke to verify. Yoshi wouldn't have told me because he would've thought that I would rush right over there and gotten myself killed.

If things had gone as I had figured, Duke or one of the members of his Dog Patrol would be keeping an eye on Molasses' house. If so, Rocky the pit bull wasn't the one on that particular duty – he had been following me since I'd left my house this afternoon. I had discovered him when I was on my way to Willy's house and he had stuck with me ever since. That was fine with me. If I was running headlong into a confrontation with Nails, I was okay with another pit bull backing me up.

The first hint that something was wrong came when I was around the corner from my destination. Chuck shot around the corner and was coming right at me with a frantic expression on his adolescent cat face.

"Hey!" he yelled as soon as he saw me, "Get to Molasses house! Duke's in trouble!"

"What's wrong?" I asked. Then thinking better of it I said, "Never mind! I can go see for myself. Rocco's following me; go tell him what's going on!"

I took off. As soon as I turned the corner I saw something that made the fur on my neck stand straight up. Molasses' home was four houses down from the corner and on her front lawn I could clearly see Nails, Fusco and Geech about to attack Duke. Duke was backed up against a tree with the three dogs surrounding him. That was bad enough but the topper was that I could see a very frightened Molasses in the tree directly above the dogs.

I thought that I was going at full speed before but I kicked it up another notch and headed for the dogs. Nails and Fusco jumped Duke. He was able to fend Fusco off but at the cost of leaving himself open to Nails. She sunk her teeth into his underside. By that time I was right there and bracing to launch myself at Nails and Duke.

Now I knew full well that even as mad as I was, a Pit Bull, a Doberman and whatever Geech was were unlikely to be intimidated at the sight of a twelve pound, extremely handsome orange cat but I was still going to hit them with everything I had and hope that I could knock Nails off of Duke. Maybe I did look pretty ferocious –Geech and Fusco's eyes widened and they turned tail and ran. Then I heard pawsteps coming rapidly behind me and I remembered that Rocky had been following me. I eased up just a little and Rocky raced past me and launched himself at Nails.

Nails had seen him coming and released her grip on Duke's side so that she could face Rocky's attack. When he landed on her, they got tangled in a whirlwind of teeth and paws and they forcefully rolled into the tree behind them.

Their impact shook the tree causing Molasses to fall off of her branch.

Everyone knows that cats always land on their feet. Not always. Not if the fall is less than six feet. And not if they're so stressed that their body's natural instincts don't kick in. Molasses either didn't have time to right herself or the situation was too much but either way she fell from the tree and hit the hard, dried out ground head first.

I got to her fast. She was lying on her side and I wasn't sure if she was breathing or not. She was definitely unconscious. I swallowed hard and tried to keep calm. I have a vague recollection of fighting going on around us but I couldn't tell you what was going on with the dogs. My focus was entirely on the beautiful, injured cat in front of me. Only a few sounds got through to me: I could hear some humans coming out of their houses and yelling at the dogs and also the whine of approaching sirens.

It took me about half a second to realize that standing there and staring at her wasn't really helping the situation. The woman I lived with had once watched a first aid training video while I was in the room and I tried to remember if I had learned anything useful from it. Molasses's mouth was open but she didn't seem to be breathing. I took a deep breath, put my mouth against hers and breathed out. That got no reaction. I tried the same maneuver again while also using my forepaws to massage her chest. Still no reaction. I had nothing better to do so I kept at it.

After I had performed this procedure six times I took a second to look around. Nails and her crew were gone. Duke was lying prone by the street curb surrounded by cops and animal control guys. More and more neighbors were coming out of their houses to see what was happening. I took a deep breath and turned my head back towards Molasses. But it was a wasted breath. Molasses coughed a couple of times and opened her eyes.

"Wh- What are you doing?" she asked.

I felt a huge smile break out on my face. "I think that I just brought you back to life."

She coughed again and then smiled weakly. "Geez, what you won't do to get a kiss."

Apparently a human had been watching us. "Hey! I think that cat just gave that other cat CPR!"

That caused a stir and people began to approach us. "Okay, kid." I told Molasses, "The people are coming to take care of you. I'll see you later." I gave her a wink and took off down the street.

After I'd gone a safe distance I looked back. Mo was being attended to by a couple of policemen. I was pretty encouraged that she was going to be alright so I headed home.

****

I got back to my house at about 5:30 just before our people got back from work and daycamp. I kept to myself and away from Yoshi until the family all gathered in the kitchen for dinner. He and I headed for the master bedroom so that I could report. Yoshi jumped up on the bed and took his usual listening position, lying at the head of the bed. I took a seat on the floor beneath him and reported. I told him about my chats with Willy and Sunshine. Then I described how I'd figured out where Chuck had gone that afternoon and how that led to Molasses's house. As I described the chaos that I encountered I tried to keep the anger out of my voice. I don't think that I succeeded but Yoshi didn't seem to notice. He seemed to be asleep but I knew that he was listening to every word that I uttered and filing the information away in his head until it was needed.

Usually when I finished reporting I sat and waited for any questions that he might have. This time I just stood up and headed for the door.

"Excuse me!" The sharpness in Yoshi's tone indicated that he hadn't expected me to leave. I turned around and glared at him.

His eyes narrowed. "I have a few questions is you don't mind. Do you have any information as to the condition of Duke and Molasses?"

"Not really. I assume that they were taken to the vet's office on Brice road. I'm going to drop by there tonight and check up on them."

He grimaced at the thought of someone willingly going to the vet. "Be sure to give them my regards. I don't suppose that Nails was apprehended?"

"I heard that her buddies Geech and Fusco got picked up and are now cooling their paws at the Animal Control facility. Any more questions?"

"Just one. Are you angry with me?"

That seemed so obvious that it didn't need an answer. I didn't say anything.

"Apart from your report, you haven't said a word to me tonight. Are you giving me the silent treatment?"

I just looked at him.

"I suppose that you're mad that I didn't tell you that I'd theorized that Nails might be staying at Molasses's house. By the way, I'm very impressed that you figured that out. Your reasoning skills are really coming along."

I had to remember that I was mad so that my face wouldn't show any sign of the pride that I felt from that compliment.

He continued. "I'm sure that you want to know my reasons for not telling you –"

"Hey!" I interrupted, "Its kinda hard to give you the silent treatment when you keep speaking for me. I do have a couple of things to get off of my chest. If you and I are going to continue doing whatever it is we do, we need to make a new rule. I know that you like to withhold information from me when we're on a case. I assume that its so that you impress me when you make your grand explanations of whatever mystery it is we're investigating. But from now on, if you have even the slightest inkling that Molasses might be in harm's way, you're going to tell me. If you don't agree to that right now, you and me are through."

Yoshi blinked a couple of times. "If I don't always tell you all of my suppositions it's not from a need to impress you. Sometimes it's more of a training exercise. You need to learn to make logical leaps and see patterns that aren't obvious. I'm not getting any younger and –"

"You certainly aren't. I can hear your joints make this weird cracking noise whenever you jump up on the bed."

He rolled his eyes. "I'm glad that your sense of humor has returned. The other reason that I may not be completely forthcoming is your welfare. If I had told you what I suspected you would've rushed over there and gotten yourself killed. So I had Chuck tell Duke that I thought that Nails might be staying at Molasses's house. I realize that things didn't turn out optimally but I don't think that things would've gone any better had I informed you of my theory."

"Whatever" I replied. "The next time you have any theories, suppositions or whatever involving Molasses, you will tell me or you and I are through. Understood?"

Being the elder cat, it was usually Yoshi who would dictate things to me. He didn't seem to care much for the tables being turned but he nodded and murmured, "Understood. Now back to business. I have another question. This cat Sunshine, how was she acting?"

Apparently we were putting any hard feelings behind us. "Well she was kind of weird. " I answered. "She was nervous and laid back at the same time."

"Did you notice any drooling or shortness of breath?"

"You mean from the heat? No, no more than normal for a young female in my presence." Yoshi just stared at me until I said, "No, no drooling or shortness of breath. Why?"

Yoshi smiled at me. "Nothing that has anything to do with Molasses."

I was still a little annoyed with him or I wouldn't have said what came next. "It doesn't matter to me. I know exactly what's going on."

Yoshi had been laying down for our entire discussion but this got him to sit up. "Really? And what exactly is going on?"

This was dangerous. I thought that I had a handle on what was going on but if I was wrong he'd never let me forget it. On the other hand if I was right and I had worked this out before he had, I would never let him forget it. I had to buy time to make sure that I was correct. "I don't think that I want to tell you my theory at this point of the investigation. How's that feel?"

"I see," he said in a condescending tone.

I felt myself getting angry again. "You don't believe me? How about a bet? If I guess who actually attacked Sophie before you do, I want a full apology for not telling me that Nails was at Molasses's house, delivered from you to me in front of Molasses, Duke, Chuck and whoever else I decide to invite."

"I think that you know full well that my acceptance of your new rule in our relationship was a tacit apology."

"I don't know what tacit means but I'd like an apology where you actually say 'I'm sorry'".

Yoshi rolled eyes and then said, "What happens if you're incorrect?"

I didn't really have an answer for that. "Uh, we shake paws and pretend that nothing ever happened?"

"I think not. How about if when this is over, if whatever you've surmised is incorrect, you'll owe me a favor."

I snorted. "Are you kidding? My life consists of doing you favors."

"Yes, but you always have the ability to say no. This would be a favor that I would call on whenever I like. It might be something that you might not want to do and that you would have to do without question."

It didn't seem like a good idea to agree to something so open ended but I was too far gone to back down at that point. "Fine."

"And how do you propose we determine the winner?"

"When I go to see Duke tonight I'll tell him what I think is happening. When everything is over, he'll be able to tell you that I was right." With that I turned and left the room.

He didn't look very worried.

CHAPTER 6

I set out for the animal hospital at about 7:30. I wasn't going to be missed at my house as my people were hanging out with the neighbors. Since today was the third of July there would be no work or school tomorrow and they'd probably stay out late.

Having a vet office slash animal hospital two blocks over and five blocks up from my house was probably very convenient but I wouldn't know. Due to Yoshi's horrible carsickness, we actually had a vet who came to our house to give us checkups. The only time I had ever visited this vet office was when I'd had an emergency case of impacted anal glands (which I will never mention again).

The animal hospital was in a two story brick house that looked like it was about a hundred years old. I had a working knowledge of the layout from the time I'd been there so I thought that I had a pretty good idea of where Molasses might be located. Getting inside was easy as someone had left a first floor window open. Once inside, I found that the layout hadn't changed much from the last time I was there. The first floor had a big reception area and waiting room in front and some examination rooms and a lab to the rear. I was guessing that Molasses and Duke were upstairs where they kept the animals who were staying overnight. As far as I could tell there were only two people holding down the fort at the office that night, a man and a woman. The two of them didn't seem to be doing much work, just chatting in the reception area.

I snuck up the back stairway and into a hall that was lined with doors. I took the first door on the right which was conveniently ajar. The room that I stepped into was painted a garish light green color and was lined with big cages filled with a few lethargic looking canines. I was in the dog room. Since most of the cages were empty it was pretty easy to spot Duke.

I walked up to his cage and greeted him in a cherry tone. "Hey Duke, how are you feeling?"

He didn't look overjoyed to be in a cage but he looked healthy enough except for the big bandage covering his belly. "Hey, kid. I've been worse."

Robert J. Smith

"That's weird because you've certainly looked better. By the way Yoshi told me to give you his regards."

Duke eyed me suspiciously. "What's that supposed to mean? What are regards?"

"I don't know. I don't think it's an insult. He actually seemed concerned when I told him that you got hurt."

He snorted. "Hurt? I just got nicked up a little. Don't go telling anybody that I got hurt."

It took some effort and I almost strained my face muscles but I succeeded in not rolling my eyes. I just sat down and asked, "Is there anything that I can do for you?"

"Don't worry about me kid. I figured that you'd be out working on Percy's case."

"Well since you've mentioned Percy's case, I have a small favor to ask."

"Hmpf!" Duke grunted. "What can you do for me, huh? What do you want?"

298

"Well I bet Yoshi that I've figured out what's going on with Percy. I just need to tell you what I think and then later when everything's sorted out, you can tell Yoshi that I called it."

"A bet, huh? What are the stakes?"

"If I win Yoshi has to apologize for not telling me that Nails was hiding out at Molasses' house."

"You want him to apologize for not letting you get your fool self killed?"

The way he put that made too much sense so I decided to ignore it. "Well can I tell you my theory or not?"

"Ha! You've got a fancy theory, huh? You sound more like Yoshi every day. Sure tell me your theory. This place is boring the heck out of me, I need a good laugh."

"Whatever. Look, I know Nails has been in the neighborhood shaking down animals for life's necessities."

Duke got serious. "Is that so?"

"Yeah, both of those witnesses that you sent me to talk to were each visited by Nails."

"Which fits in with what Molasses told me. That mangy pit bull was committing extortion right under my nose!"

"Well she had just gotten started," I said with genuine sympathy. "You would've shut her down soon enough."

"I'm slipping."

"Yeah, you're what? Eight years old? You're getting up there. It's really no surprise that you're starting to lose it in your declining years."

He emitted a low growl that immediately let me know that kidding or not, I probably didn't want to go too much further in that direction. "Ok, so the pets that I talked to were very accommodating under the threat of being hurt or having their house burned down or whatever but what if Nails tried this on Sophie and she said 'no'?"

"You tell me."

"Nails would've attacked her. Not enough to kill her but enough to intimidate her into doing what she was told. Then Nails would tell her to keep her mouth shut about who had jumped her. Sophie would know that if she blamed Percy, everyone would probably believe her."

Duke nodded. "Sounds good. What about the witnesses? Did they say that Nails was the one who attacked Sophie?"

"Willy claims that he didn't see anything and Sunshine definitely states that Percy was the attacker. But they both caved instantly to Nails' demands. If they were told to cover up her crimes, they'd do it without a second thought. And who wouldn't want to pin something on Percy?"

Duke thought about that for a few seconds. I was used to seeing him big, strong and in action. He seemed unnatural being in a cage and bandaged. I fought back an urge to open the cage door and let him out. If that's what he wanted he would have already asked me to do it.

"OK, kid you're making a lot of sense. It'd be nice if you had some evidence or facts but I have to agree with what you're saying."

"That's right and I got there before Yoshi. The student has surpassed the master."

That got a derisive snort out of Duke. "Right. So does Yoshi think that something else happened?"

"I don't know what he thinks. Probably nothing. I told him what Willy and Sunshine told me but he's going to talk to them tomorrow. He's too lazy to form an opinion until he sees them. Of course if Sunshine's lying about seeing Percy attack Sophie maybe Yoshi can get the truth out of her."

"What about Sophie?" A thin, high feminine voice said, "Is she lying?"

Apparently my conversation with Duke was entertaining the other dogs in the room. Without looking around I said. "I hope that I'm not being rude and speaking too softly. Is everybody getting all of this?"

When I did turn to look at the other caged dogs, I noticed that two cages down there was a black Pomeranian. I grinned at her, "You're Sophie, aren't you?"

She did not grin back. "Yes I am and I think that I know who I was victimized by, thank you very much!"

I walked over to Sophie's cage. "Sorry but I've known Percy for a while and he's always been an all bark and no bite kind of dog. It's hard to believe that he finally attacked somebody that wasn't me."

I was in front of her cage at this point and she didn't seem thrilled to see me. She was a classic cutesy kind of dog. The kind whose people would dress her up and spray perfume on her. She didn't look all that pretty at that particular moment. Her side was patched with bandages and gauze but a corner had fallen loose and I could see a deep scratch peeking out.

"I don't care what's hard to believe. That awful bulldog has been threatening me and making fun of me for years! Of course he did it! Why would I lie? Who are you anyway?"

Duke had somehow let himself out of his cage and had walked up behind me. He was moving slowly. "Settle down, Sophie. Percy says that he didn't do it so I had to ask Gatsby here to talk to the cats that live across the street from you. Just to see what they say happened."

"I heard you say that they told you exactly what happened and you think they're lying."

She seemed pretty adamant but I wasn't ready to give up on my theory just yet. "Well Sophie, let me ask you a couple of questions. Have you seen a pit bull named Nails?"

"I don't think so."

"Are you sure? Both Willy and Sunshine say that they were visited by her."

"Yes, I'm sure! I've never heard of any pit bull named Nails. It was Percy who did this to me and I'm not interested in talking about any pit bulls! Do you know that I have scratches that go an inch deep? I'm lucky that no major organs were punctured! I can't believe that I have to sit in a cage, fighting for my life while some strange cat accuses me of lying! Unbelievable!"

Yoshi would sometimes quote a human named Shakespeare and while I did my best not to listen, some things still got through. The quote that was coming to my mind at that moment was 'Methinks the lady doth protest too much'. I was now sure of two things, that she was lying and that I was right about who had attacked her.

I didn't hear any people coming but somebody might decide to check on all of the barking that Sophie was doing. It seemed like a good idea to get out of the dog room.

I turned to Duke. "I don't think I'm getting anywhere here. Do you know if Molasses is in the next room?"

"Yeah," Duke said, "Her and another cat. I snuck in to see her as soon as most of the people had gone home. She's doing fine. They're just keeping her here for observation. I'm surprised that you came to see me first."

"I didn't mean to. Anyway you take care of yourself. You better get back in your bed and get some rest."

"Aw, don't worry about me kid. It's going to take more than Nails to take me out. Even at my advanced age."

305

I laughed and exited the same way I'd come in. There was no one in the hallway and I didn't hear any footsteps on the stairs. The man and woman were probably still downstairs yakking with each other. There was a room opposite from the one I'd just departed and the door was slightly open. I walked into a room very similar to the one I'd just departed except that it was painted bright yellow, the cages were smaller and there was an open window in the corner.

"Gatsby!" Molasses called out. She was in a wire cage on a counter that was about five feet off the floor. There was a bunch of empty cages in the room and there was a black and white cat fast asleep in a cage at the far end of the room.

I leapt up onto the counter that Molasses' cage was on. "How are you feeling?"

"I'm fine. I had a little headache at first but now I'm ok. They should let me go home soon. Of course since my people are in Disneyland, I don't know when I'll be able to go back."

"I'm just glad that you're ok. Now I can yell at you. Why didn't you tell me that Nails was hiding out at your house?"

She looked slightly embarrassed. "I didn't want you getting yourself killed."

"There's a lot of that going around. Next time something like this happens, promise me that you'll let me know."

A cute smirk appeared on her face. "The next time my people go on vacation and a psycho dog decides to take over my house, I'll be sure that you're the first to know."

"Ha, ha" I said without any mirth. "Now tell me everything."

"Well she came over yesterday morning and basically told me and Butterscotch that she was taking our house until our owners got back. Then she practically dared me to tell you about it."

"Hmm. Did she say anything about what she was up to?"

"No. She didn't talk much. Most of the time they made Butterscotch and me stay outside. They let us back in when Mrs. Murphy came over to feed us. Then after she left, they ate our food and kicked us out again. They were -"

She stopped and cocked her head for a second. "Sorry, I thought I heard someone coming. Anyway Nails and her friends weren't nice houseguests. I don't know what their plans are. And I hope that you don't find out. Let that other pit bull take care of her."

"You mean Rocky? I'm not sure he's tough enough. He needs to hang around me a little more and pick up some pointers."

"Not funny." She said sternly. "If I find out that you got into a fight with Nails, you better believe that I'll kill any part of you that she doesn't!"

Before I could answer we both heard footsteps coming up the stairs. Molasses whispered, "OK, I love you. Now get out of here and don't go do anything stupid!"

I jumped down from the counter and headed for the window. "I love you too. I'll see you when you get out."

The footsteps were in the hall and getting closer. I jumped up on the windowsill, looked back at Molasses and gave her a wink. Then I exited through the window and was on my way.

CHAPTER 7

Nothing notable happened until around three in the afternoon of the next day. It was the Fourth of July which was apparently a big deal. Since it was on a Friday our people were leaving town to spend the three day weekend with relatives. I spent the morning hoping that Nails would hear about this and show up to try to take over my house.

Yoshi had spent the morning either reading or napping and was now sitting in the kitchen window waiting for our first guest. He was in a bay window on the side of the house and I was sitting outside in the grass beneath him. Willy showed up right on time, exactly at 3:00. He approached from the front of the house. For some reason he looked a bit nervous. He wasn't shaking or anything obvious but he definitely seemed like he was worried about something. When he saw me he said, "Here I am. Where's Yoshi?"

I nodded up towards the window. Yoshi was sitting in the window but Willy had to concentrate to make him out. The bright sunlight outside combined with Yoshi's black body behind a screen made it difficult to see him clearly. Yet another way for Yoshi to be mysterious.

"Good Afternoon Willy. I'm Yoshi. I was flattered to hear about your action figures. They sound very creative."

Willy didn't faint but he didn't seem that far away from passing out. "Uh, thanks! Or I mean, you're welcome! Wait, I mean thanks."

I figured that I'd better say something before he stammered himself to death. "I think that what Willy is trying to say is that he's honored to talk to us and what can he do to help?"

Willy shot me a dirty look and said to Yoshi, "He said that you wanted to talk to me."

Yoshi gazed down at him. "Please have a seat."

Willy settled down in the grass next to me. "Ok."

"As you're well aware, Percy the bulldog who lives across the street from you has been accused of mauling Sophie, another dog who lives across the street from you. The fact that you can

310

usually be found in your front window makes you a likely witness but you say that you happened to be away eating when the attack occurred. Is that true?"

"Yes."

"Fine. That's the answer that you've given multiple times and I'm not going to attempt to change your position. How well do you know Sunshine?"

"Sunshine?" The change in topics seemed to confuse Willy.

"Yes, Sunshine." Yoshi repeated patiently. "Your next door neighbor."

"I don't know her that well. She's only been here for a few months. Whenever she's outside she's usually in her backyard. Since I stay in my front window I don't really see her a lot."

"But you know her by sight, right?"

"Well, yes."

"How well do you know Sophie? Since she lives across the street, I assume that you see more of her."

311

"Yeah I know her. She's very nice for a dog. Sometimes she would come up on my porch and talk to me."

Yoshi took a moment for a huge yawn. When he was done he asked, "What did you and she typically speak about?"

Willy pounced on that question with the enthusiasm of a kitten going after a crinkle ball. "She always talked about Percy! He was constantly bullying her and telling her that she wasn't tough enough to be a real dog. I heard him tell her that if she ever stepped a paw on his property that he'd tear her apart."

"Is he meaner to Sophie than he is to anyone else?"

Willy paused for a moment to think. "No, he'll yell at anybody who gets too close to him."

"Have you ever actually seen Percy attack anyone?"

"No. But he's made it clear that if he ever gets off of his chain, there's going to be a bloodbath."

Yoshi rolled his eyes. "And they wonder why I never leave my house."

"Oh please" I sighed. "You're the only one in this neighborhood who has nothing to fear from Percy and you know it."

Willy looked at me with question marks in his eyes.

"Percy loves and admires Yoshi," I explained.

"Really?" Willy clearly didn't believe me.

Yoshi said, "I did him a favor a few years ago and he's appropriately grateful."

Willy nodded but it was apparent that he still didn't believe Yoshi. He turned to me and said, "Well I know that Percy hates your guts."

I grinned. "Sometimes when I'm bored I like to go to his house, stand just beyond the reach of his chain and make observations about his looks, his attitude, his poor hygiene and his -"

Yoshi interrupted me. "That brings up an interesting point. Willy, do you have any idea how Percy would have gotten off of his chain?"

313

"No. It's happened before though. His people just get a thicker chain."

"And on those occasions has he ever actually mauled anyone?"

"Not that I know of. But with the way he acts it was only a matter of time. I really don't get why you guys are trying to help him."

I answered him. "We've got to have something to do. Or I do anyway. Yoshi could get by just sleeping, eating and reading but I need something to do."

Yoshi's eyes narrowed. "This is a very serious situation. If Percy didn't do what he's been accussed of and we don't establish that, there could be two negative consequences. One, Duke could banish Percy from the neighborhood for something he didn't do and two, if Percy didn't commit this attack then someone else did. Someone who is still at large and able to attack others."

If that was meant to persuade Willy to change his story, it fell flat. Willy just sat there looking nervous.

"What's with you?" I asked him. "You look more nervous than a dog at a vets convention."

He looked at me as if I were an idiot. "Don't you know what today is?"

"Friday?"

"No! It's the fourth of July!"

I acted like I didn't know what he was talking about. "And tomorrow is July fifth. So?"

"So tonight they'll shoot all those horrible lights and noises into the sky! I'm going to be a wreck all day and then I'll probably spend all night under the bed!"

Yoshi was sympathetic. "The humans have their insane celebration without any thought to the distress it causes us."

"Oh I don't know," I said, "I kind of like the fireworks. They can be pretty awesome."

Everything went quiet for a few seconds as Yoshi and Willy looked at me as if I'd said that I prefer dry dog food to tuna.

Yoshi broke the silence by telling Willy that fireworks were unlikely to do him any harm.

"I know, I know." Willy said, "But it's still going to freak me out!"

Out of the corner of my eye I saw Rocky the pit bull cop walk past the front of our house. Was he following Willy around or was he keeping an eye on me? My attention was brought back to the matter at hand by Yoshi asking Willy if he had any questions for us.

"No," Willy replied. "I guess I'll be getting back to my house. It was an honor to meet you."

He waited for Yoshi's reaction. When it became obvious that there wasn't going to be one, he turned towards the front of the house and trotted off.

When Willy was out of earshot Yoshi said, "Did you notice that pit bull that's been going back and forth in front of our house?"

"You mean Rocky? Yeah I saw him go by once."

"He's passed by three times. He's actually pretty skilled at not being seen. I'm not sure that I like the idea of a stealthy pit bull. They're formidable enough without being able to sneak up you. What does he want?"

"I don't know. Maybe he was following Willy. Maybe Duke sent him to see what you and I are up to. Duke doesn't think that you're always up front with him."

Yoshi smiled. "He's correct."

I could've said that in that case Duke could get in line behind me but I held back. That's right, the cat had his own tongue.

Sunshine came to join us a few minutes later. She trudged up slowly. With the way the heat was still beating down on us her lack of energy wasn't surprising. She took a seat in the grass between me and the house. After flashing me a quick smile she looked up at Yoshi and said, "What's up?"

Yoshi cocked his head at her. "I have no idea how to answer that question."

"What?" She said.

"He's not into colloquialisms." I told her.

"What?" She said again.

I looked at Yoshi. "Can you get started? And try to keep your words below six syllables."

Yoshi's eyes had never left Sunshine. "Thank you for coming. My name is Yoshi. You spoke to my associate yesterday regarding the attack on Sophie."

"Yeah and I told him what I saw. Do you need to hear what I told him?"

"No, Gatsby told me what you said and you seemed quite positive."

"Quite." She said in a slightly mocking tone.

Yoshi ignored her tone and continued. "I'm curious about something Gatsby mentioned. He said that you have a garden. Is that true?"

"Yeah, man. I have some plants in the back of my girl's garden."

Yoshi didn't even flinch when she called him 'man'. "There's nothing like getting your paws dirty. What exactly do you grow in your garden?"

"Just plants." She replied.

"Really? I can't imagine that's it's been easy with this weather we've been having."

"It's ok. You just have to make sure that they get lots of water."

You would have thought that changing the topic from Sophie to gardening would have put Sunshine at ease but she seemed to get more tense.

Yoshi kept going. "It's a shame that you can't be more specific about what you're growing."

"I didn't think that you wanted me here so that we could chat about my garden."

"Actually I'd much rather talk about what happened to Sophie but you're obviously lying about that."

"What?" was all that Sunshine could reply.

"You heard me. I know that you're lying about what you saw but I don't have a way to force the truth out of you so I thought that we may as well discuss horticulture."

That statement got Sunshine's dander up. Well I don't actually know if she had a problem with dander or not. I just mean that she got mad.

"Look man, I know that everybody around here thinks that you're the smartest cat in creation but I think that you're out of your mind. I'm not lying!"

Yoshi just stared at her. "As you like it. I just want you to realize that I don't think that you're lying. I know it for a fact."

"So do I!" A voice boomed out. Percy the bulldog walked out from behind our house. It wasn't a surprise as we'd all heard him coming but his entrance did make for good drama.

"Oh I might have known!" Sunshine sighed. "Here comes the perp!"

"Who you callin' perp, you twerp?" Percy growled. "You need to stop saying that you saw me attack Sophie. You know that I've never hurt anybody."

Sunshine snorted. "You've certainly changed your tune. Up till now all we ever heard from you was how you were going to hurt us. Now you're a big teddy bear. Well it's not going to work. I know what I saw and when Duke gets back, he's going to throw you right out of the neighborhood! Later, man!" She got up and walked off toward the front of the house.

I gave Yoshi a questioning glance. He shook his head. We both shifted our gaze to Percy who had taken a seat in the exact spot in the grass that Sunshine had just departed.

When he'd gotten comfy Yoshi asked Percy, "Is there something that we can do for you?"

"How are you guys doing with my case?"

I answered before Yoshi could say anything. "Not so hot. You're probably going down."

He turned to me with a horrified expression on his face. When he saw the grin on my face the horror turned to rage. "This isn't funny, you little fleabag!"

Yoshi wasn't amused either. "Gatsby, unless you have something to contribute-"

"I do. I have a question for Percy."

Yoshi inclined his head slightly, a signal for me to proceed.

"Well Percival," I began (He hates when I call him Percival). "You've been roaming around pretty free and easy for the last few days. Up until now you've usually been chained up in your backyard. How are you getting loose?"

"None of your business!"

Yoshi sighed. "Actually I've been wondering the same thing. We can help you but you need to be forthcoming."

Percy was quick to answer Yoshi. "It's pretty easy. When my man's sprinklers go off, I just stick my head in the water and then I can slip out of my collar."

"And he doesn't notice?"

"As long as I'm in the backyard when he's looking for me, he doesn't care."

"Interesting," Yoshi murmured. "Where exactly were you when Sophie was attacked? I know that you've said that you were in your backyard but I find that hard to believe."

"I was over on Ericson Street. I was trying to track down a weird smell."

"Did anyone see you?"

"Nah, I wouldn't be in so much trouble if somebody had seen me. Do you think that Duke will really kick me out of the neighborhood?"

"It seems likely unless we can establish your innocence" Yoshi's voice became stern. "I've warned you that your belligerent attitude would lead you to your end."

Percy's gaze dropped to the ground. "Yeah, I know".

After about a millisecond of solemn contemplation his head popped back up. "But I came here to tell you something. That ugly pit bull came to see me."

"Nails?" I asked.

"Yeah, Nails. She came right into my backyard and told me that if I gave her half of my food every day, she could guarantee that nothing bad would happen to me or my house. She said that she was like an insurance policy.

"You're in good paws," I muttered to no one in particular.

Yoshi ignored me. "What was your response?"

Percy got a nasty look on his face. "I laughed in her face. I told her that I could guarantee that something bad would happen to her if she didn't get away from me."

"How did she take that?"

"She didn't like it. She just said that she hoped my man was paid up on fire insurance."

I probably should have saved my breath but I couldn't resist giving Percy some advice. "If I were you, I'd go see the Dog Patrol. I know that Duke is laid up but Rocco or Preston should be able to help you."

"Ha! I don't need any help against some puffed up pit bull!"

Having disposed of my ridiculous suggestion, Percy turned back to Yoshi. "I figured that you might want to know about Nails."

Yoshi let loose with a long, extended yawn and then said, "Thank you for sharing. We'll let you know if we discover anything significant on your case."

Percy's tone was the softest I'd ever heard from him when he asked, "Do you think that I did it?"

Yoshi rolled his eyes. "That's not the problem. I'm sure that you're innocent. The problem is proving it. Or at least making a convincing argument that someone else did it. Which might be easier if it wasn't for your attitude."

"I know, I know. If you get me out of this, I'll be a nice dog. I swear!"

I got a nice laugh out of that. Percy whipped around at me and said. "What are you laughing at? I can change!"

"I'm sure," Yoshi reassured him. "Why don't you go work on your self-improvement while Gatsby and I try to sort out your problem?"

Percy cheered up. "That's cool. If anybody can do it, it's you!"

With that he got up and walked towards the street. After he was gone I said, "You may want to reconsider our bet. You don't seem too motivated."

Yoshi yawned again.

I continued, "You could've kept Sunshine here a little longer and gotten more out of her. I know what you're up to. With our people gone for a few days you figure that you can just sleep uninterrupted around the clock. The faster you get rid of the witnesses, the faster you can get back to bed."

"Be careful of drawing conclusions based on incomplete evidence." Yoshi said. "Although that does describe my approach to this current problem."

"You've drawn a conclusion?" I asked in the most casual tone that I could muster.

"Yes but I don't have a shred of evidence. My theory is based entirely on my knowledge of animal psychology and physiology."

Whatever. I didn't need to take any Psyche 101 classes to be sure that Nails was suspect number one.

"Is there some kind of evidence that you need me to get?" I asked.

"No. I do have a suggestion if it won't interfere in your own investigation."

"What is it?"

"That pit bull is still lurking about."

"Rocky?"

"Yes. Whenever he gets tired of our house, I want you to follow him."

"Do you think he knows something?"

"Maybe . In any event, he's been following you around often enough. Let's turn the tables."

I liked that suggestion. "OK, I think that sounds good."

"Good." With that he turned around and jumped down. I heard the thump he made on the kitchen floor and his pawsteps as he went off to his nap.

CHAPTER 8

I ran to my backyard so that I could run across the back of the house and go back up front on the opposite side. Hopefully Rocky wouldn't be expecting me to emerge on that side. When I got to the front of the house I peeked out from behind the corner. I could see Rocky's butt showing from behind the tree near the street. I stayed put and kept my eyes on his backside.

It was a waiting game. I was assuming that he was waiting for me to leave so that he could follow me. If he didn't see me, he'd either figure that I was staying inside or that he had missed me leaving. Either way he would himself leave at some point and then I would tail him.

Characteristic of his species, he was persistent. It was nearly an hour before he gave up and trotted away. After a few seconds I went after him.

In case I haven't been clear up to this point, it was hot! Despite the sidewalks being scorching hot, Rocky trotted on them as if he owned them. I followed at a safe distance but I kept to walking on lawns. Before too long it was obvious that we were headed to Percy's neighborhood. As soon as we got in the vicinity, Rocky went towards Sunshine's house. When he got there he walked across her front yard and dived under a hedge. This caught me off guard so I had to turn around and go back a couple of houses until I found a tree to duck behind. When I peered out from behind the tree I could no longer see Rocky in the hedge.

Of course it came as no surprise when a couple of minutes later, Rocky came up from behind me and asked, "Why are you following me?"

"You fascinate me." I said without bothering to turn around and face him. "I want to know more about you. What's your favorite food? How do you get your flea treatment applied? What kind of bones do you like to chew?"

"Mostly cat bones."

I had to turn to face him in order to make sure he was kidding. "Whatever. What are you doing over here?"

"You wouldn't come out and play so I thought I'd come over here and see if Nails was around. Come on, it's cooler in the bushes."

I followed him back to the hedges in front of Sunshine's house. It was a good vantage point as it was directly across the street from Percy's house. It would be hard for anyone to see us and most importantly it was shady.

The first hour or so was uneventful. Percy's house was quiet. His people were probably out. Rocky and I didn't seem to have much to say to each other until he broke the silence. "I don't get the whole cat detectives thing."

"What's not to get?"

"Most cats that I know aren't cut out for this kind of work. They're kind of lazy and full of themselves."

"Really? Well if you're going to get insulting, I'd say that most of the dogs that I've met are way too dumb for this kind of work."

"But dogs do all kinds of policework. There's bloodhounds, there's policedogs, there's dogs in the Army and lots of guard dogs. How many cats do any of that kind of stuff?"

"Probably none," I admitted. "Cats don't let people order them around. Nobody's telling me what to do unless I –"

I stopped in mid-sentence. I noticed Percy trotting down the sidewalk towards his house. He was moving slow and he was panting with his tongue hanging out of his mouth. When he got to his driveway he turned to approach his house. He got eight pawsteps up his driveway and then stopped in his tracks. Nails the pit bull appeared at the other end of his driveway and was approaching Percy.

Rocky tensed up as soon as he saw Nails.

"Hold on." I told him, "I want to hear this."

Percy had stopped but he didn't back up at all as Nails walked right up to him. Their paws must have been burning from standing on the hot driveway but neither one of them looked uncomfortable. They were too busy looking mad.

Percy spoke first "I thought that I told you to keep away from my house!"

Nails wasn't impressed. "So you want to take me up on my offer or what?"

"Forget your offer. I ain't afraid of you. You don't even have your boyfriends around anymore."

"Those two were dead weight," she growled. "I don't need them. But you need me. Bad stuff could happen if I'm not on your side."

Percy wasn't buying it. "I told you to get out of here!"

"Fine." Nails replied, "But don't say you weren't warned. I hope you don't have any trouble tonight."

She walked past Percy and took off up the street.

I was about to exit the hedges and follow her when Rocky growled, "Hold on!"

"What? Let's follow her. I thought that you owed her some bruises."

"She'll be back. Isn't that your little friend over there?"

Looking in the direction that Rocky was indicating I saw Chuck the kitten approaching from the end of the street. For a second I thought that he might be there to give me a message from Yoshi but he wasn't looking for me or sniffing the air to get my scent. He went straight to Willy's house.

Rocky shot me a questioning glance. I shook my head. I didn't know what Chuck was doing but I didn't want to call out to him and give up my hiding spot. We could hear Chuck climb up Willy's front steps and begin a conversation with Willy. Chuck and Willy's voices were nowhere near as loud as Percy and Nails' had been so while I could hear them talking, I couldn't make out what they were saying. Their conversation didn't last long. After a few minutes we could hear Chuck leaving Willy's front porch and heading for the backyard.

"Where's he going?" Rocky whispered.

"I don't know," I answered. "Yoshi probably sent him."

"For what?"

"I don't know. Maybe he has more questions about Sophie."

"What kinds of questions?"

I rolled my eyes. "Stop me if you've heard this before – I don't know. Yoshi and I aren't working as closely as we usually do."

"Why not?" This was one inquisitive dog.

"We have a bet on which one of us can figure out what really happened to Sophie. I figure that Nails actually jumped her then told everybody to blame Percy. I'm thinking that if I can talk to Nails, I can probably annoy her into confessing."

Rocky looked doubtful. "So what does Yoshi think?"

He timed it exactly so that he and I both said, "I don't know!" at the same time. Then he flashed a wolfish grin at me.

"Wonderful," I muttered. "The hottest day of the year and I'm sitting in a bush with the world's only funny pit bull."

Those were the last words spoken for a while. Chuck came back out from Sunshine's backyard and headed across the street to Percy's. He had passed right by me and Rocky without noticing us. I was going to have to work on his observational skills.

Rocky and I went back to our stakeout. After the flurry of activity we had just witnessed not much else happened for the next hour or so. We sat beneath the hedge in silence as the skies began to get darker.

Willy emerged from his house at about the time that night hadn't quite fallen but was definitely getting ideas. He took off down the street, heading north.

"Where's he going?" Rocky asked. "I thought that he never left his house."

"I don't know." I replied, "It's weird because earlier he made such a big deal about how much he was going to hate the fireworks tonight."

"Yeah, the park's just a couple of blocks over. The fireworks will be right over this neighborhood. I can see how that might be annoying. Maybe he decided to go someplace else."

The words were hardly out of his mouth when we saw Sunshine come out of her backyard and head in the same direction as Willy. Rocky gave me a hard stare. It wasn't hard to guess what was going on in his head. Chuck had been here earlier and now both Willy and Sunshine and left their homes and were headed in the direction of my house. He had to be thinking that Yoshi was up to something and that I knew what it was.

If Rocky did suspect something he didn't say a word. He just looked at me like he was stopping himself from saying some things that might hurt my feelings. Then Percy came out from his backyard and trotted of in the same direction that Willy and Sunshine had gone.

I smiled at Rocky and said, "Now you know perfectly well that if you ask me where those three are going I'm going to say that I don't know. Which is actually the truth."

"Give me your best guess."

"Well I would guess that Yoshi called them because he has more questions about Percy's problem. Anyway it really doesn't matter. Nails attacked Sophie. I'm going to wait for her to show up and when she does I'm going to get some payback."

His dog eyebrows shot up. "Payback?"

"Yeah. Nails put my girl in the hospital."

"And you're out for revenge? You, a twelve pound cat against that one dog wrecking crew?"

"Don't sell me short." I said.

"Yeah, I've been told not to do that. If we do run into Nails will you let me help you out?"

"Sure, just try not to get in my way."

That seemed to amuse him and we went back to silence. It wasn't a long lasting silence, as about fifteen minutes later Rocky asked me, "Did you hear that?"

"Hear what?"

Rocky tensed up. "I thought that I heard something at Percy's house. I'm going to check it out. You stay here!"

Really? The chances of me following a dog's orders were about the same as me laying an egg. I followed him as he emerged from Sunshine's hedges and headed across the street.

It was twilight and everything was quiet. As we crossed the street and approached Percy's house a sickening thought occurred to me. While Rocky and I had been watching the front of the house, nobody had been watching the back. If Percy had been around, he would've raised a lot of noise if anyone came within his vicinity. But if Nails had waited for him to leave and then came back, the back of his house was completely unguarded. Rocky or I should've taken a post in Percy's backyard. I had to blame Rocky for that oversight. Otherwise it would be partially my fault and that couldn't possibly be right.

We went straight to the backyard. When we got to the back door Rocky stood still and listened. There were faint sounds coming from inside the house.

Rocky glanced back at me, not seeming surprised that I hadn't stayed put like he had told me. "Is Percy the only pet in this house?"

"Yep, Percy's an only pet." I whispered back. "I hear some animal in there that's not supposed to be in there."

"I'm going in." He said and then entered the house through the doggy door.

I followed him inside. As soon as I entered the house I was confronted by two horrifying scents. I could smell both the stench of Nails and the odor of something burning. We were in a back hall that I thought probably led to the front room but the smoky smell was coming from a doorway on my right. Before we could properly investigate the smell, we heard a sound coming from up the hall. Without a word, Rocky bolted up the hall. This time he didn't even bother to tell me to stay put and I was thankful. If he had ordered me not to follow him, I would have felt obligated to ignore him. Since he hadn't issued any commands I was free to do as I wished.

I went through the doorway to my right and found myself in the kitchen. It was a grim sight. The place was a mess. There were dirty dishes piled up in the sink, old mail stacked on the counter and dust bunnies in the corners. Also the room was on fire. Flames were spreading all over the kitchen floor and it looked like they had originated from a dishrag that was burning in the center of the room. If that wasn't enough, all of the gas burners on the stove were turned on and they were set to high. What had happened seemed obvious. Someone had turned on the stovetop burners, set fire to the dishrag and put it on the floor. Looking around I could see another flaming dishrag next to the square wooden table in the corner and one more next to the cabinet under the sink. Both the table and the cabinet were starting to catch fire. There was no sign of Nails and I was no longer able to catch her scent with all of the smoke overloading my senses. I had seen a fire extinguisher near the back door but that wasn't going to do me a lot of good. The idiot humans always designed their tools so that you needed thumbs to operate them.

I was wondering if it would be possible to put out the fire by turning on the faucets on the kitchen sink and overflowing it when I heard a loud thud and a yelp from the room in front of the kitchen. Wonderful. As if the fire wasn't enough, now I had to go see what was going on with Rocky. The other side of the kitchen actually went right into the front room but I didn't feel like dodging the flames on the floor so I backed out the doorway that I had entered and ran up the hall in the direction that Rocky had gone.

I emerged into the living room and it looked kind of spooky. The only light in the room was coming from the fire in the kitchen but I could still make out a sight that made me gasp. Rocky was sprawled out on the floor next to an end table and he looked out of it. A wrought iron lamp was on the floor beside him and I'd bet that the sound I'd heard was the lamp bouncing off of Rocky's head before it hit the floor.

Crouching on top of the end table that the lamp had presumably come from was Nails with a mean expression on her harsh face. Somehow she had knocked Rocky on the head with that lamp and now she was about to pounce on him and finish the job.

"Hey Nails!" I yelled. "Why don't you go stick your face in that fire and improve your looks!"

She fixed her mean eyes on me. "I was hoping that you'd show up!"

She jumped down from her perch on the end table and began to slowly approach me.

I honestly don't know how I constantly find myself in these situations. Behind me the fire in the kitchen was getting more intense and the smoke was getting thicker throughout the house. In front of me the meanest pit bull I'd ever encountered was coming at me with the intent to do serious bodily harm.

We had reached the point in the evening when just about the only light in the house was coming from the kitchen fire. The house had an open layout and only a counter separated the kitchen from the room we were in so as Nails walked towards me, I could see the fire dancing in her eyes. I stood my ground.

While she wasn't bothered by the fire, Nails did seem to be taken aback by my attitude. "Why aren't you running?" She demanded.

"Behind me the house is on fire. In front of me a pit bull wants to tear me to pieces. I might as well stay put."

She gave me a look that indicated that she thought that I might be having some IQ trouble.

If I had timed things correctly, I might have a chance to survive. But I needed to stall her for a few more minutes. "Can I ask you a question?"

"Sure." She was in a generous mood.

"Did you attack Sophie, the dog that lives next door?"

She snorted. "No. I don't know anything about that. You need to worry more about who's about to attack you."

That wasn't good. She had no reason to lie and in fact if she had done it, she'd probably be bragging about it. So she hadn't mauled Sophie.

She'd gotten about two feet away from me and stopped. Then she looked over her shoulder to make sure that Rocky was still in la-la land. Rocky did seem to be stirring a little but it was obvious that he wasn't going to be much help in the next few seconds.

bacon. When I hit them, they stay —"

Suddenly a loud ear-splitting whistle sounded from outside followed by a deafening boom. The Fourth of July fireworks had begun. I had expected them to start a little earlier but they still started in time to save my neck.

Nails freaked out. Her eyes bugged out and she lifted her head and began to frantically bark at the ceiling. I took the opportunity to turn around and run back down the hall. Nails regained her composure and came after me. I led her down the hall and into the back entrance to the kitchen. The smoke and fire in the kitchen had gotten worse. The wooden cabinets above and beneath the counters were fully aflame and there were few parts of the floor that weren't on fire. This was not a room that you'd want to run into if you had a choice but with Nails on my tail I didn't so I did.

There was enough of the kitchen floor not on fire that I could navigate a path to the doorway that led back to the living room. I was hoping that Rocky had come around enough to help me out. When we'd gotten about halfway through the kitchen another whistle sounded and another boom rattled the house. Again, Nails was startled and stopped chasing me for a second. This was a bad place to stop. I don't know if a cinder fell on her or if she had brushed against something that was burning but she was suddenly on fire. As you might expect the flames that appeared on her back freaked her out even more than the fireworks had. There was a look of wild panic on her face as she bolted past me and ran into the living room.

"Roll on your back!" I shouted at her when I entered the living room. The fire hadn't yet reached this room but the smoke was thick. My eyes were watery and it was getting hard to see but I saw Nails follow my advice. Rocky was back on his feet and seemed okay. "What's going on?"

"Nothing much!" I yelled. I had to yell as the fireworks were now going off in earnest and on top of that, we could hear sirens approaching. "I just saved your butt. Now do you want to carry on with your nap or should we try to get out of here the way we came in?"

A human voice from outside the front door yelled, "Hey! Is anyone in there?"

Apparently people had finally noticed that the house was on fire.

"Let's go!" Rocky snapped.

Nails had rolled herself over towards the front door and with all the smoke in my eyes it was hard to see if she was still on fire. I could hear that she was still apoplectic. She obviously wasn't going to be much of a threat. Rocky and I made our way back through the hall and were able to get to the back door. I let Rocky exit first through the doggy door. Before I left I heard the front door being smashed open.

"Holy cow!" A man shouted, "There's a crazy dog in here!"

'He doesn't know the half of it' I thought to myself as I headed out the doggy door. Rocky and I were able to get out of the backyard and circle around to the front of the house without anyone noticing. I had never appreciated how wonderful fresh air could feel. We didn't go back to our hedge but we did go across the street to watch the goings on. It was quite a sight. The night was not only lit up by the fireworks that were still going off in the sky but by the flashing lights on the two fire trucks that were parked in the street. The firefighters were able to extinguish the fire pretty quickly once they realized that Nails was too messed up to pose any kind of danger. She was pretty subdued once she was out of the house and the firemen kept her under control until Animal Control showed up to take her away.

After everything seemed settled, Rocky said, "I'm not sure what happened back there, but thank you. I'm never going to understand how a scrawny little cat like you got the better of a dog like Nails. How'd you do it?"

I smiled. "There's a lot of animals around here that are bigger than me, stronger than me and smarter than me but you've never in your life met a cat that's luckier than me."

CHAPTER 9

Rocco accompanied me back to my house. On our way we passed quite a few people out on their porches and lawns but apparently they were too busy watching the fireworks to pay any attention to a cat and a pit bull walking the streets.

We entered my house from the rear, through the backdoor into the kitchen. As soon as we entered, we could tell that something was up. I could smell that there were other animals in the house and the scents were familiar.

Rocky looked at me. "So this is where Willy and Sunshine and Percy went. Why?"

"I don't know," I answered, "Let's go find out."

He followed me down a stairway and into the basement. My house had a finished basement and it was kind of a second living room slash office complete with a couch, a television and a desk. An interesting scene greeted us. Yoshi was sitting on the bamboo end table next to the couch. Sitting on the floor beneath

349

him was a big burly German Shepherd. It was Preston, Duke's second in command in the Dog Patrol. Chuck the kitten sat close behind him. Sitting on the floor in front of them were Sunshine, Willy and Percy. Yoshi had apparently been giving them a lecture.

Yoshi raised his eye whiskers as we approached. "You two look like you've had an interesting night."

Preston was a little more effusive. His eyes bugged out and he said, "For the love of dog! You guys look like something the cat dragged in, chewed up, spit out and dragged out again! And why do you smell like smoke?!"

I smirked at him. "Hey, it's the Fourth of July. We were out enjoying the fireworks. Up close."

Preston ignored me at looked at Rocky. "Really?"

"No, sir." Rocky replied. "We encountered Nails at a neighborhood house. She seemed to be in the middle of committing arson. She caught me at a disadvantage and Gatsby assisted me. He overcame her and the last we saw, Animal Control was taking her away."

That seemed to surprise Yoshi. "You say that Gatsby overcame her?"

"That's what I said." Rocky seemed a little annoyed.

I was more intrigued by what was going on in the living room. "So, what's up? Are we having another Q and A session?"

"It had better be more than that." Preston muttered.

That statement told me a lot. If Preston was expecting this to be more than a group interrogation, that probably meant that Yoshi was about to reveal exactly who had attacked Sophie.

I gave Yoshi a dirty look. "Having a party without me?"

Yoshi sighed. "You seemed a bit irritated with me and I had no way to contact you. So I asked Chuck to go out invite our guests over so that they would have someplace to go where the fireworks wouldn't be quite so disturbing. Did you discover anything that would affect our wager?"

"Yeah," I sighed, "I figured that Nails actually attacked Sophie but Nails denied it and she had no reason to lie so I believe her. I lose the bet."

"Not if I don't uncover the truth of this matter." Yoshi turned to Chuck. "I believe that I hear the rest of our guests coming. Would you go up and escort them down?"

Chuck sighed and then trudged up the stairs as if he'd been asked to clean out his own litter box. His teenager phase was a little annoying. I liked him a lot better when he was a bight eyed, eager to please young kitten.

Willy looked mildly annoyed and after Chuck had departed he decided to speak up. "Look, this is starting to feel weird. I really appreciate you letting us stay here where we could hardly hear the fireworks but they're probably over by now. I'm going home."

Yoshi gave him a cold stare. "Actually, I'd like you to stay a while longer. I want to speak to all of you about the incident involving Sophie."

Willy responded with a shocked "What?" while Sunshine rolled her eyes and said, "Whatever."

Willy stayed put and not much else was said until Chuck came down with our newest visitors. It was Duke, Molasses and

Sophie, the dog that was apparently going to be the subject of tonight's discussion. Duke and Sophie still had bandages on their sides but Molasses looked as good as ever. As I walked over to greet Molasses, Duke brushed past me to see Rocky and Preston. He took them over to the corner of the room by the desk where they most likely filled him in on what had been going on since he had been in the hospital.

I wanted to see how Molasses was doing but Yoshi called out, "Gatsby! I need a few words."

I spun around and headed back towards him. He jumped down from the end table and we headed to the corner of the room furthest from the Dog Patrol. I knew exactly what he wanted and I gave him a quick rundown of what had happened since I left our house that afternoon. After I was done we went back to the rest of the animals. Yoshi retook his position on top of the end table and I went and sat next to Molasses to see how she was feeling.

Yoshi gave Duke and his dogs a couple of minutes for their conference and then cleared his throat and said, "I need to speak to the room. Would the Dog Patrol like to have their meeting elsewhere? Preferably not in my house?"

Duke felt the same way about dealing with Yoshi as he did about getting a flea bath. It was an awful and unpleasant experience but it was necessary so he was going to have to grit his teeth and get through it. "We're staying right here!" he growled. "From what my guys are telling me, this has all the earmarks of one of your typical gatherings."

Yoshi wasn't intimidated in the least. "These animals are gathered here to avoid the horrible sights and sounds of the humans' annual Fourth of July idiocy. Now that it's over, I thought that I might ask a question or two about Percy's problem. I think that I might be able to clear that up."

It was Duke's turn to be unimpressed. "Based on what? From what I've heard, the facts of the case haven't changed since I've been in the hospital. I'm thinking that this is just you going on another fishing expedition without any bait."

Percy's eyes had lit up when Yoshi had said that he could clear things up. Now he looked a little annoyed. He turned to Duke.

"Why are you arguing with him? We asked him to help. If he can tell us what's going on, just get out of his way."

"I asked him to talk to some uncooperative witnesses," Duke growled. "Not to take over and grandstand!"

I thought that this was a good time to put in my two cents. "Look Duke, from the moment you called Yoshi and me into this case, you had to know that it would come to this so why don't you just let Yoshi talk?"

"Fine." Duke grunted.

With that resolved, Yoshi addressed the room. "I think that you all know that Duke and Percy asked me to assist in the investigation of Sophie's assault. To summarize the situation, there was a particularly nasty incident in our neighborhood a couple of days ago with which you are all familiar. Sophie was mauled in her own driveway by a dog that she identified as Percy. Percy has denied any involvement. There seem to be peculiarities with the witnesses. Willy, who is never seen off of his perch in his front window, was conveniently off eating when the most action he's ever likely to see takes place. Sunshine claims to have witnessed the entire incident and definitely names Percy as the perpetrator. As does Sophie herself. The situation doesn't look good for Percy at all."

"It sure doesn't." Sunshine agreed.

Yoshi ignored the interruption. "The aspect of this case that intrigues me the most is Sophie's testimony. As a species dogs aren't quite as objectionable as they might seem. Despite all of the negative qualities of dogs, there is one undeniable positive aspect —"

"Hey!" This time the interruption was from Sophie. "What negative qualities?"

It probably would have been better if she had just let that go. But she had been foolish enough ask the question so Yoshi answered.

"Dogs don't have the decency to use a litter box. They don't clean themselves. Their slavish toadying to humans is disgusting. They often smell like — "

This time he was interrupted by all of the dogs in the room who all started barking unintelligible protests. After a moment he was able to talk again. "Please! I was only answering Sophie's question. This will all go quicker if I'm not interrupted. Now I'm going to mention something that I admire about dogs. They are extremely guileless. Usually they are truthful in all matters and their emotions are easily discerned from their facial expressions. In short, dogs don't lie. What you see is what you get."

"Yeah," Duke growled. "As opposed to cats who can be crafty, deceitful and – "

"I thought that we'd agreed to no more interruptions." Yoshi interrupted. "As I was saying, dogs are poor liars. Sophie, can you once again tell us what happened when you were attacked?"

All eyes went to Sophie. Her nervousness level shot up to about a 9 out of 10. "I've already told you all what happened."

"I know." Yoshi said. "But I'd like to hear it again here in front of the accused. Do you object?"

She didn't say a word. She looked at Duke. He just grunted, "Go ahead."

Percy put in his two cents. "Yeah, I've been wanting to hear this story!"

Sophie gulped and looked around at all of the animals looking at her. After a minute of that she just put her head down and started whimpering.

Duke wasn't sympathetic. "What are you doing? This isn't how you were acting the other day! What's going on?"

Sunshine said, "She's probably afraid to talk in front of Percy."

Yoshi nodded. "Perhaps. But the sixth amendment of the Constitution of the United States guarantees that anyone accused of a crime has the right to face their accuser. I realize that this isn't court of law but the principle is sound."

"Yeah," Duke agreed. "Sophie, there's nothing to be scared of. Rocky, Preston and I are all here and we won't let anything happen to you."

Sophie just sat there looking nervous and not saying anything except an unintelligible whimper.

Yoshi murmured, "Percy didn't do it, did he?"

"Here we go!" Percy shouted.

Sophie continued to whimper.

Duke turned to Yoshi. "Since you've turned Sophie into a blubbering mess, would you like to tell us what's going on? If you're telling us that you know that Percy didn't do it, then who did? Nails?"

Yoshi glanced at me so I spoke up. "I just talked with Nails and she says that she didn't do it."

Willy was incredulous. "And you believe her why?"

I rolled my eyes. "Try paying attention. We've already established that dogs don't lie."

Yoshi added, "Not unless there's a very compelling reason. The question that we need to consider is –"

Rocky's eyes bugged out as he interrupted Yoshi. "Hey! I just remembered something! Percy, your house was on fire!"

"What?" Percy said.

"Me and Gatsby caught Nails in your house after she started a fire. That's when she told him that she didn't attack Sophie!"

Percy snarled at me. "You never forget anything! Why didn't you tell me that my house was on fire?"

I gave him my most winning smile. "I don't like you. Besides the fire had been put out by the time we left."

Percy didn't even bother to bark at me anymore. He just looked at Yoshi and said, "I know that you're about to tell everybody who jumped Sophie but I've got to go!"

Yoshi just nodded and Percy took off.

Duke gave Yoshi a wary eye. "You got anything else that clears Nails other than the fact that dogs don't lie?" He took a sidelong glance at Sophie and added, "Well, mostly."

"There is one other thing. Gatsby, when you were at the hospital, didn't you get a look at Sophie's major wound?"

"Yeah, her bandage was loose. She had some obvious clawmarks."

Everyone's eyes involuntarily travelled to Sophie's bandage. There was nothing much to see. The dressing had been reset and her wound was now fully covered.

"So Duke," Yoshi continued. "If we were to remove your bandage, would we also find clawmarks?"

"No, Nails sunk her dirty teeth into me. What does that have to do with –?" He stopped and you could almost see the gears turning in his head. "If Nails or one of her cohorts had attacked Sophie, they would've led with their teeth not claws!"

No one had anything to say to that. Sophie was still a mess. Both Willy and Sunshine were busy avoiding eye contact with anyone else in the room. Duke and the dogs were staring at Yoshi.

Duke kept talking. "Claws, huh? Are you thinking a cat's behind this?"

"Let me ask you a question." Yoshi relied. "You heard me speak of the usual honesty and sincerity of dogs. What would make a dog like Sophie lie?"

Duke growled, "You're telling it."

"Well, pride was the first thing that sprung to mind."

Willy was confused. "Pride? What does pride have to do with anything?"

Yoshi yawned and then answered. "I think you'll find that pride has a lot to do with animal behavior. For instance what if a small, well groomed dog was constantly made fun of for not being tough enough by her loutish next door neighbor? If this dog was attacked and seriously wounded by a housecat, wouldn't her pride prevent her from telling the truth about her assailant?"

Duke was staring at Sunshine and Willy as he asked, "Is that what you're saying happened?"

"From the facts that I've been presented, it seems like a likely supposition."

Duke wasn't convinced. "How's that? I have an eyewitness that says she saw the whole thing."

"Yeah," Sunshine said. "I saw Percy do it! Why are trying to get him out of it?"

"Because I'm a cat." Yoshi responded. "And as such I'm a natural hunter. Right now I'm hunting the truth and I'm pretty sure that the truth is that you're covering up for Willy. Isn't Willy the one who attacked Sophie?"

This took Sunshine off guard. She just sat there with her mouth open. Willy wasn't much better. "What?" he howled.

Yoshi's tone got hard. "You heard me. I'm sure you did it due to the –. "

"No!" Willy yelled. "I didn't do it! Sunshine did! It was Sunshine!"

Sunshine turned to face him. "Shut up you idiot! He doesn't know anything!"

At that point a lot of animals started talking at once. Duke and his dogs were confusedly barking at each other, Sunshine was berating Willy, Sophie was still whimpering and Molasses gave me a wink and said, "Yoshi just said that Willy did it. If it was Sunshine, does that mean that Yoshi was actually wrong?"

Even with all that noise going on Yoshi heard that. "No I wasn't wrong. I was falsely accusing Willy in the hope that he would break down and admit to what he had actually seen. I spent all afternoon developing a false motive for him and then he goes and blurts out the truth before I even get out half of it!"

I tried to placate him. "It's okay Yoshi. We can all sit here and pretend that we didn't hear what Willy said and then you can tell us this motive that you concocted. Or on the other paw maybe you can just get over it and explain why a hippie tortie would jump a Pomeranian."

"I didn't jump anybody!" Sunshine yelled.

Duke wasn't buying it. "Oh please the cat is out of the bag, if you'll pardon the expression. Now are you going to tell us what happened or are you going to let Yoshi tell us?"

"Whatever!" she sniffed.

"Fine. Yoshi?"

Yoshi, still perched on the end table looked annoyed. I knew that he was irritated at being constantly interrupted. "It isn't enough that I've named her and that from her body language, she practically confessed? Very well, Sunshine would you be open to answering a few more questions?"

A scowl appeared on her cute tortoiseshell face. "No. I've had enough questions about what happened to Sophie."

"That's fine." Yoshi smiled. It was the same smile that I'd seen when he'd had a mouse cornered. "I agree that subject has gotten tiresome, but that's what we're talking about right now so if you don't want to talk maybe someone else will." He looked at Willy. "Willy, I'm pretty sure that Sunshine was the attacker. Are you ready to tell us what you saw?"

Willy didn't say anything. I jumped in. "Willy, come on. I thought that you liked Yoshi and me. Help us out."

He gulped. I'm sure that he could feel Sunshine glaring at him. He looked at Yoshi. "You were going to accuse me!"

"I was trying to force you to tell the truth. Now I'm just asking."

Willy sighed. "Fine, I'll tell you."

Robert J. Smith

Sunshine hissed, "You better keep your mouth shut!"

Duke growled at her, "No, you shut up!"

Willy got himself together. "Okay. Here's what really happened. Sophie was in her backyard at first and I could hear Percy yelling at her and -."

"What was he yelling?" Duke asked.

"Oh, the usual. That she's a wimpy little Pomeranian and not a real dog like him. He was always picking on her like that. Then I saw Sophie come out onto her front yard and then as quick as lightning, Sunshine shot out from her backyard, ran across the street and started beating on poor Sophie."

"How long did it last?"

"It was over before it started, just a bunch of growling and slashing and then Sunshine ran away. She left Sophie on her front lawn, all messed up. I actually came out of my house and went to see if I could help. I stayed with her until some people got there."

Yoshi asked, "Did she say why she had been attacked?"

"No. She just kept asking me not to tell anyone that a cat had done this to her."

Yoshi looked at Sophie. "Why not?"

At this point Sophie stopped whimpering and began to fully cry.

Yoshi said, "What's wrong with you? Do you need a nap?"

Naps were Yoshi's answer to everything. However what he said gave me an opportunity for a little wordplay and I couldn't resist. "No, you should never let lying dogs sleep!"

Everyone ignored me which was just as well. Willy continued his testimony. "I think that she's embarrassed that a cat did that to her. I can only imagine what Percy would say."

"Is that why she blamed Percy?" Yoshi asked.

"Probably. I'm sure that she doesn't like him and it wasn't like she'd think that anybody wouldn't believe it."

Duke snorted. "I didn't believe it!" Having established that he added, "I'll buy all of that but what did Sophie do to make a little tortie cat go nuts like that?"

Sunshine was still glaring at Willy but spit out, "This little tortie didn't do anything. Willy's lying!"

"Sophie?" Duke growled.

She was finally ready to talk. "Yes! Yes! Sunshine did it! I didn't want anybody to know that I was beaten up by a cat."

"So you blamed it on an innocent dog?" Duke couldn't quite believe what he was hearing.

"Innocent?" Her eyes lit up. "Ha! What happened to me was what he threatened to do to every animal in the neighborhood. If you ask me, I was doing us all a favor by blaming him. If you would just kick him out of the neighborhood, you'd be doing us all a favor!"

If Percy was still there he might have paused to soberly reflect on the feelings that his behavior had aroused. Although probably not, he was kind of a jerk.

Duke was not happy. "When this is over, we're all going to have a little talk about the importance of telling the truth to the Dog Patrol. But I still don't get what set Sunshine off. Anybody want to enlighten me?"

Everybody looked at Sunshine. "I didn't do anything and I'm not talking about this anymore!" She stood up as if to leave.

Duke opened his mouth presumably to tell Sunshine to sit back down. Before he could say anything, Yoshi said, "You're right. That has become boring. How about we change subjects? How about horticulture?"

That surprised Sunshine. "What?"

"Gardening. When we spoke earlier we were interrupted before you could tell me what plants you grow in your garden. Can you tell me now?"

She answered in a tone that suggested that she expected Yoshi to jump all over whatever she said. "Nothing special. Just some flowers and stuff."

"Any particular kinds of flowers?"

"No, I just like pretty flowers."

"No doubt," Yoshi replied. "I'm partial to orchids myself. Gatsby, what was the most prominent flower in Sunshine's garden?"

"I don't know the technical name," I answered. "But it was kind of a purple and white flower with very small petals."

"Can you describe it in more detail?"

Not a problem for a cat with my observational skills. "The leaves were triangular with serrated edges and the stems were square. Some of the leaves seemed petty chewed up."

"Weird looking plant." Rocky muttered.

"Yeah," I agreed. "But the weirdest thing is how green those plants were. Even with all of Sunshine's care and watering, most of the plants were looking brown and dry but not those."

"Yes," Yoshi said, "Nepeta Cataria is a xerophyte."

"What's zero who?" I asked.

"I'm sorry," Yoshi explained. "A xerophyte is a plant that is highly drought resistant."

"That's wonderful." Duke growled. "I'll keep that in mind if I ever need to take the SAT. What's Nepeta Cataria and what does it have to do with the matter at hand?"

Yoshi smiled. "Nepata Cataria is more commonly known as catnip. I believe that Sunshine has been growing her own catnip."

Everybody looked at Sunshine. All she had to say was "So?"

Duke was doing some heavy thinking. "So are you saying that she was hopped up on drugs?"

"Catnip isn't technically a drug." Yoshi said. "But the chewed leaves do indicate that someone had been using them for recreational purposes."

Duke said, "I thought that catnip made you guys mellow. Why would she attack anybody?"

"That depends on the cat." I answered. "It doesn't do anything for me but some cats get relaxed, some are unaffected

371

and a few get really nasty. Sunshine could be one of the few, the proud, the crazily aggressive."

Sophie had stopped crying when Yoshi had brought up gardening. She turned to Sunshine and asked, "Is that what happened?"

Sunshine had a hard time meeting Sophie's eyes. After a few seconds she stopped trying. "Yeah. Sorry. My people put that plant in the backyard and I love it but it makes me kinda mean. I've scratched up my girl and her mother and then you. Sorry."

"Sorry doesn't cut it!" Duke growled. "Here's what's going to happen: Me and my boys are going to Sunshine's house tomorrow and dig up the catnip plants and get rid of them. And then I ought to banish Sunshine from this neighborhood."

All of the animals in the room let out a gasp. Kicking an animal out of their home was the most severe form of punishment that Duke could impose. The Dog Patrol would escort a criminal to the edge of the subdivision and tell them not to come back. This was pretty traumatic for the animal as well as the pet's owners, who would assume that their pet had run away.

This punishment was usually reserved for repeat offenders or violent, out of control animals.

"What?" Sunshine was shocked. "No!"

"Relax," Duke said. "This was an isolated incident. Or it had better have been. I'm thinking that a more appropriate punishment would be five or six weekends of community service."

Sunshine looked relieved. She didn't seem overjoyed at the prospect of picking up litter around the neighborhood for the next month and a half but it was better than banishment.

Duke continued, "I don't know what's worse, hopped up cats attacking dogs or the dogs lying about it and blaming other dogs. Anyway, me and Percy and Sophie are going to have a little talk. I'm going to make sure that he lays off of Sophie."

Then he gave Sophie a hard stare. "Also you and me are going to talk about how much I like being lied to."

"I'm sorry."

"Yeah," Duke replied. Then he looked up to Yoshi. "Am I missing anything?"

"Just the part where you all get out of my house."

Duke rolled his eyes. "Whatever. Actually if Sophie, Molasses and me don't get back to the animal hospital soon, we're going to be missed. It's time to break this party up."

Molasses seemed to be the only animal disappointed to hear this. I reassured her that I'd be by to visit her the next day. Everyone else departed in a somber mood.

After they were all gone Yoshi and I went to the kitchen. We didn't put the lights on upstairs so the house was completely dark but that didn't bother us. I went to my food bowl next to the fridge and got a few bites of cat food. Yoshi hopped up onto the windowsill. The window was half open and Yoshi took a couple of sniffs of the night air. "There's still a lot of gunsmoke in the air." He stated.

"Yeah, the people like their lights and noise." I said between munches.

After I'd swallowed a couple of mouthfuls I said, "So, those books you were reading. Which one was correct? You said that there were two different viewpoints."

He looked a little surprised. "Well, neither. Or both. The facts of history are always open to interpretation."

"So what made you think that it was Sunshine? I get that Sophie had been scratched up and that made a cat a likely suspect, but why Sunshine?"

Yoshi smiled. "Something that she said during your first talk with her was suggestive."

In my mind I reran my initial conversation with Sunshine. The answer came to me almost immediately. "When I asked her to come talk to you, she said that it might look bad if she didn't. What would look bad? Nobody had accused her of anything. Why would she be worrying about looking bad if she didn't do anything?"

"As I said, it was suggestive. I wasn't sure of anything but I had a working hypothesis and I thought that I might as well give it a try."

"So I guess I owe you a favor now."

A big smile spread across his face. "Oh yes you do."

"Fine. What is it?"

"Oh it's not for today. Or tomorrow. It may not be for years from now. It may not even be until after I've passed away. You'll just have to be patient."

That's how he left it. I had no idea what this favor was or when he'd call it in but it's always stayed in the back of my mind. So ever since then, whenever he catches me looking at him in a certain way he knows exactly what I'm wondering.

THE END

PETECTIVES EXTRAS

INTERVIEW WITH THE PETECTIVES

Yoshi and Gatsby did an interview with Truffles, the cat from the blog "Melissa's Mysteries, Mochas & Meows". Truffles is a prolific interviewer of literary animals but she had her hands full with the Petectives:

Truffles: Hi everybody. Today I'm interviewing Yoshi and Gatsby the two cat detectives from the Petectives books. Hello Yoshi and Gatsby. Can you tell us about yourselves and how you came to live with your family?

Gatsby: I'm a handsome, smart and funny orange cat. Actually you're pretty cute yourself. Are you named after the chocolate? I'll bet you're just as sweet.

Yoshi: Gatsby! Restrain yourself. Truffles is here to interview us, not be subjected to your cheap advances. If I may answer the question, I am a black cat who enjoys reading and napping. Our humans brought me home from a pet store eight years ago when I was a kitten. Gatsby?

Gatsby: I'm an orange cat who was born in the woods as a member of the Lightning Clan feral cats. I was declared their chosen one and am destined to rule over all –

Yoshi: Gatsby!

Gatsby: OK, OK. Our family picked me up at the Pets without Parents animal shelter three years ago. Before that I was a street kitten. Which must be where I picked up my street smarts and roughish charm.

Truffles: I see that your stories are written by Robert J. Smith. Is Robert your daddy?

Yoshi: Daddy? Actually we think of Robert as more of an annoying roommate. In human years, I'm almost fifty years old; I'm hardly going to refer to him as 'Daddy'.

Gatsby: But what about his wife? We call her Mommy, don't we?

Yoshi: Well of course she's Mommy, don't be silly.

Gatsby: Rob's very useful though. I can tell him about our cases and he'll write them up and publish them for me.

Truffles: Why did you guys decide to be detectives?

Yoshi: We both find the life of a housecat to be a bit on the boring side and need the stimulation that detective work provides. I enjoy the mental aspects of the work while Gatsby craves the physical parts of the job.

Gatsby: Actually he sends me out to go out and do all the work while he sits at home and thinks about what I dig up. Yoshi's definition of thinking consists of sleeping and reading books. Anyway, cat detectives are definitely needed where we live. We're in a nice suburban neighborhood but you can't imagine all the bad stuff that goes on in the animal community. Everything from extortion to attempted murder. But when a pet around here gets into trouble, they know who to call.

Truffles: Yoshi, I've heard that there's prejudice against black cats. Have you experienced any of that?

Gatsby: Oh boy, here we go.

Yoshi: I'm glad you asked that. I'm sick of the human's irrational, superstitious fear and loathing of black cats. It's probably based on jealousy of our sleek, regal appearance. But no matter the cause, during the weeks preceding Halloween, I'm afraid to step a paw out of my house for fear that some demented human will harm me!

Truffles: But I understand that you never leave your house at any other time of the year.

Yoshi: Certainly not. I have food, books and a nice warm place to nap. Only someone with the subnormal intellect of a dog would leave the comfort of their home for any reason whatsoever.

Gatsby: Hey wait a minute! You're constantly sending me out of the house.

Yoshi: That's true. So Truffles, do you have any other questions?

Truffles: Let's talk toys. Do you guys prefer catnip mice or a laser light?

Gatsby: Laser light. Catnip doesn't have much of an effect on either of us but chasing something down is right up our alley.

Yoshi: Speak for yourself. I prefer a good book.

Truffles: Well Yoshi, this is a book friendly blog. What are you currently reading?

Yoshi: Right now I'm in the middle of the latest No. 1 Ladies Detective Agency novel, "The Minor Adjustment Beauty Salon" by Alexander McCall Smith. I'm also reading "Hallucinations" by Dr. Oliver Sacks. It's another of his fascinating examinations of the human brain.

Gatsby: Those sound incredibly boring. Look, let's be honest. Nobody should read anything but Petectives books. They're brilliant, they're funny and I get a decent cut of the profits.

Truffles: Is there anything else that you guys want to say?

Gatsby: Buy our books! Buy five or six copies of each! I need treat money!

Yoshi: From now on, I'll be doing these interviews by myself.

Truffles: Thanks guys.

Petectives Profiles

Yoshi

<u>Real Life:</u>

- AKA: Crazy Yoshi

- Black cat; 16 pounds

- Bought at a pet store in a mall in Troy, MI

- He was given an Asian name due to his resembling a Siamese cat when he was a kitten. He grew out of that appearance but kept the name.

- Yoshi loves salty snacks such as french fries, potato chips and pretzels. He's been known to swat nacho chips out of people's hands so that he can jump down to the floor and recover them.

- Refuses to ride in a car. If someone can survive his teeth and claws and actually get him into a cat carrier and into the car, he will get so horribly carsick and noisy that it will be almost impossible to drive

<u>Fictional version:</u>

- 9 years old. Black cat; 16 pounds

- Knows how to read. Enjoys the books on his owner's bookshelves.

- Refuses to leave his house for any reason.

- Yoshi doesn't think much of dogs but has a grudging respect for Duke, the German Shepherd leader of the neighborhood Dog Patrol.

- Yoshi enjoys four regularly scheduled naps throughout the day which can never be disturbed except for extreme situations.

- Considered a legendary figure in the neighborhood. Since he doesn't leave his house most pets have never met him.

Gatsby

<u>Real Life</u>

• AKA: Philo; Catboy; Knucklehead Smith; Safety Cat

• Orange cat with light stripes. 12 pounds.

• Rescued pet; We got Gatsby at Pets Without Parents, a non-profit, no-kill, all-breed shelter for dogs and cats in Columbus, OH.

• Gatsby is usually skittish although he has been known to deliver a series of blows to dogs four times his size.

• Likes dry dog food as a snack

• He seems to howl at people doing things that he considers unsafe. This habit has earned him the nickname "Safety Cat"

• Supposedly an indoor cat but has made several attempts to escape to the outdoors.

<u>Fictional version:</u>

• Narrator of the Petectives stories.

• 3 years old. Orange cat with light stripes. 12 pounds.

• Gatsby is very intelligent but has a reckless temperament and doesn't always think through the consequences of his actions. He's prone to making risky decisions based on emotion.

• Gatsby has a very good vocabulary as a result of living with Yoshi, his housemate and partner in crime detection.

• Outgoing and friendly. Loves to get out of the house. Actually enjoys the company of some dogs.

• Something of a "ladies cat" before he met his girlfriend Molasses.

• Gatsby has a high regard for Yoshi although he would never admit it.

Duke

Duke is an entirely fictional character

• Duke is the leader of the Dog Patrol, an informal canine police force dedicated to keeping order in the neighborhood.

• 7 years old. Black and tan German Shepherd. 85 pounds. Disciplined, intelligent, honorable and somewhat cynical.

• Duke served as a police dog until he was injured in the line of duty

• Avid TV watcher – Duke's favorite show is 'The Littlest Hobo', a show about a hyperintelligent German Shepherd who travels from town to town helping people and catching criminals.

• Duke has a gruff demeanor but he's mostly friendly with Gatsby. Duke is not so friendly with Yoshi – he finds him to be arrogant and pretentious. Duke and Yoshi do have a history of working together before Gatsby was born and they both have a deeply hidden mutual respect for one another.

• Personal feelings aside, Duke respects Yoshi's intelligence and Gatsby's investigatory skills and would love for them to join the Dog Patrol but all three of them realize that cats wouldn't be likely to follow his orders. He has made them honorary members

and grudgingly agrees to work with them when necessary.

Petectives Playlist

A list of songs that I listened to while writing Petectives. Some of the songs have a thematic link to the story, while others helped me set a scene or get into the heads of the characters. There are a range of genres represented but the overall theme is sort of jazzy sophistipop.

Sister Moon – Herbie Hancock featuring Sting: Jazzed up version of the Sting song. I have never had any idea what the lyrics mean but I have imagined that they are from a cat's viewpoint.

Moondance – Van Morrison: The perfect song for the beginning of the story where cat detective Gatsby meets his lovely client on an October night under a full moon.

Black Cat – Janet Jackson: Gatsby's annoyed that there are no songs titled "Orange Cat".

Everybody Wants to Be a Cat – Jennifer Ryan: Slow, jazzy version of the theme song from the Disney classic "The Aristocats".

Watching the Detectives – Elvis Costello: The big band version from the album "My Flame Burns Blue". You can't get any more detectivey than this.

Who's Johnny? – El DeBarge

Somewhere in the World – Swing Out Sister

Peter Gunn – Art of Noise: No detective story should be written or read without this tune playing in the background at some point.

La Luna – Matt Bianco: Yet another jazzy moon song.

After All – Al Jarreau: A love song for Gatsby and Molasses.

Pink Panther Theme – Bobby McFerrin: Another cool detective song. This one with a cat connection in the title.

Heaven Only Knows – Swing Out Sister

Warehouse – Dave Matthews Band: I pictured this playing when Gatsby and Molasses are exploring the old abandoned house that turns out to be far more dangerous than they suspected.

What Is Hip? – Tower Of Power

Don't You Worry 'bout a Thing – Stevie Wonder

The Big Eye – Rusty Zinn: Rockin' blues tunes with extremely paranoid lyrics.

Someone To Watch Over Me – Ella Fitzgerald

King Of Pain – Inner Circle

Petectives: Christmas Party Playlist

A list of songs that I listened to while writing Petectives: Christmas Party. Some of the songs have a strong thematic link to the story, while others helped me set a scene or get into the heads of the characters. Forget all that, its Christmas music! Who doesn't like Christmas music?

The Christmas Song – Nat King Cole: This was the first song on a Christmas album that my mom would play while she made Christmas cookies. It's not Christmas for me until I hear this song fifty or sixty times.

What Christmas Means To Me – Stevie Wonder: The first thing that you hear is the drums and bass and you know that you're listening to classic Motown. Then the jingle bells kick in and you know that you're hearing a Christmas song. Then Stevie Wonder starts singing and you get one of the best Christmas songs ever recorded.

I Heard the Bells on Christmas Day – Frank Sinatra

Sweetest Thing – New Voices of Freedom (featuring Adriane Mc Donald & George Pendergrass) – This

Gospelled up version of the U2 song isn't a Christmas song (Although it is from the soundtrack of the movie 'Scrooged'). The song inspired the relationship between the Zabisco and Missy characters in Petectectives: Christmas Party.

Happy Holiday (Beef Wellington Remix) – Bing Crosby: Dusty old Bing Crosby Christmas song remixed with a modern dance beat. Weird juxtaposition that actually works.

Cool Yule – Louis Armstrong: All of the fun of the holidays in pure undiluted form.

Celebration – Kool and the Gang: Not a Christmas song but definitely one of the all-time great party songs.

Rudolf the Red-Nosed Reindeer – Ella Fitzgerald and Bing Crosby: Here's how this version ends: "If you keep your nose a red, red rose. If you keep your beak all pink and sleek. And if you keep your snooze maroon because, You'll go down in history." Brilliant.

Christmas Is Coming – Vince Guaraldi Trio: This jazz melody is from the soundtrack to "A Charlie Brown Christmas". That whole CD should be the sound track to Petectives: Christmas Party but it's already taken.

Christmas Must Be Tonight – Robbie Robertson: Rock retelling of the Nativity.

My Favorite Things – The Supremes: I'm not normally a big Rodgers and Hammerstein fan but Diana Ross really sells this version. I don't know if Ms. Ross actually likes schnitzel and noodles but I totally believe it when she belts it out here.

This Christmas – Donny Hathaway

A Merrier Christmas – Diane Reeves: A little known Christmas song composed by jazz genius Thelonious Monk. A musical interpretation of an idyllic American Christmas experience.

Sleigh Ride – Ella Fitzgerald

White Christmas – The Drifters: Classic do-wop interpretation of the holiday standard.

Robert J. Smith

Petectives: Under Fire Playlist

A list of songs that I listened to while writing my cat mystery novel, Petectives: Under Fire. The story takes place on the Fourth of July during a heat wave so there's lots of music related to the summertime and hot weather.

Heat Wave – Martha Reeves and the Vandellas

Hot Fun in the Summertime – Sly and the Family Stone

Stoned Soul Picnic – Swing Out Sister

Summer in the City – Lovin' Spoonful: When you hear this song it immediately evokes the feel of a sweltering hot summer day.

Little Willy – The Sweet: According to Wikipedia, this song is about a stray cat that hung around the garage where the band members practiced.

New Age Girl – Deadeye Dick: I was listening to this song when I wrote the chapter featuring the character, Sunshine the hippie tortoiseshell cat.

Fire – Ohio Players

Lies – Jonathan Butler

Gimme Some Lovin' – Sam and Dave: Somehow I've always heard this song as "Gimme Summer Lovin'".

Why Can't We Be Friends? – War

In the Summertime – Shaagy featuring Rayvon: Reggae/Rap reworking of the Mungo Jerry classic.

Summertime Blues – Eddie Cochran

I'll Take You There – BeBe and CeCe Winans

Love Rollercoaster – Ohio Players: That's right, there's two Ohio Players songs on this playlist!

Will It Go Round In Circles? – Billy Preston

Summertime – Billy Stewart

Walk Us Uptown – Elvis Costello and the Roots

Summer Breeze – Isley Brothers

Bang Bang – David Sanborn

ABOUT THE AUTHOR

Robert J. Smith is the agent of Gatsby the cat. Smith's
duties include:
- translating and transcribing Gatsby's adventures
- Managing Gatsby's business affairs and public relations
- Litter box maintenance.

Made in the USA
Charleston, SC
11 November 2016